Take Me, Break Me

Pierced Hearts, Book One

by

Cari Silverwood

Early praise for Take Me, Break Me

"An intriguing and wonderful insight into a beginning Dom."
Cherise Sinclair – author of the Club Shadowlands series.

"…both HOT and thought provoking. I love those kinds of books."
Candace Blevins – author of the Safewords series.

Disclaimer

This book contains descriptions of many BDSM and sexual practices but this is a work of fiction and as such should not be used in any way as a guide. The author will not be responsible for any loss, harm, injury or death resulting from use of the information contained within.

Acknowledgement

There are a great many people who have helped me to grow the ideas behind this story into a book. I'd like to say a big HUGE thank you to Sorcha Black, who held my hand while I knocked out the early version. More thank you's for beta reads go to Mj, Katrina Whittaker, Ekatarina Sayanova, and Bianca Sarble (my friend and up-and-coming author). Last of all I wish to thank Candace Blevins and Cherise Sinclair for their beta reads and critiques and wonderful encouraging words.

Because without them, Klaus would have driven me crazy.

ঞ Chapter One ঞ

Jodie

The contrast between the view from the café and the kinkiness we were planning made me want to laugh in a slightly demented way. Below us, waves washed up the beach then retreated, leaving foaming ripples. Diamond-lace reflections from the gentled parts of the blue, blue sea blinded me – jaw-dropping scenery – and here I'd just signed a document that gave the man opposite me permission to mind fuck me into the next century.

I squinted as a blast of wind came up off the beach and rattled the umbrella shading our table. At least Klaus had a suggestion of handsomeness about him with his short, dirty-blonde hair that could tug at your fingers like bristles on a brush, and the no-nonsense Germanic bone structure of his face. I imagined few women dreamed of being captured by a brute with a pot gut and bad teeth. Klaus would look good on film. We could edit if his acting was awful. Or mine. Only I wasn't sure how much I'd be acting.

No matter how much preparation and thinking we'd done, this whole exercise was foreign territory.

I took another swallow of my coffee frappe and set it on the little round glass-topped table. My fingers were cold. So were my lips and a spot in the center of my chest.

"You're insane. You know that don't you?" Klaus regarded me without bothering to move from his casual position in the wicker chair. Only the mild narrowing of his eyes betrayed...something. He was probably totaling up expenses, though I knew my idea disturbed him.

"Of course." I mimicked his coolness and smiled. Inside I was going *sign, sign, sign.* To do this, I didn't really need him to sign, because I trusted him, but he needed this. He'd only do this with everything under control, and with t's crossed and i's dotted.

The day I'd raised this idea came to me in vivid detail. I'd been so nervous my chest had seemed wrapped in steel. Breathing was hard to do simultaneously with wondering how he'd react, or what he'd say.

It had been tax time. Klaus always did my taxes. He'd probably cornered doing the taxes of many of the residents of Magnetic Island. This wasn't a small place, either. Though close to the mainland of Australia, it had the aura of a faraway fantasy holiday destination even after you'd lived here for years. Tropical climate, palm trees, secluded white-sand beaches, and enough hills and valleys and little roads everywhere to make it ever so quaint. Tourists were the only drawback, but even they were assets if you liked ogling them and bumping elbows with tanned cheerful people in skimpy swimwear.

Klaus's office was on the main street in Nelly Bay. If you crossed the unsealed road you'd be only a few meters from where the grass sloped down to the beach.

A breeze had riffled in through the slats of his window louvers. The roofing iron above pinged in the heat and a fan swished lazily overhead.

"Done." He reached over and dropped the final document onto the desk in front of me. "I'll see you again next year, Jodie. You've got to get more engagements, you know." He raised his eyebrows. "Or you're going to go under."

Understatement of the year. Being a comedienne and low-budget documentary maker was close to auditioning to become a street bum.

"I try." I stared back while assembling my best imitation of nonchalance. Be businesslike and this will seem less…stupid. But truly I was like one of those crazy mice on a wheel. Always, that was me. Today wasn't that different from my average day. Inside my head, I was running fast in circles, like an insane hamster, while on the outside I acted like a hip sunglasses wearing chick who'd just stepped out of the Ice Age. I'd even gotten a tattoo above my butt this year. I was pretty sure that made me badass.

"Was there something else you wanted?"

I let out that breath. *Go.* "I have an idea. Performance art of a sort. I want do a film based on me going through the experience of a capture fantasy." That blank look I'd expected. Men didn't read truckloads of erotic stories like women did. Or like I did, anyway.

"Capture fantasy?"

'Nother deep breath, let it out. I rattled out the words like I'd memorized them for a test, which I kind-of had. "It's a fantasy of a lot of women – where the protagonist of a story is captured and basically made to serve a man sexually and sometimes in other ways. So she becomes his slave or at least under his control. Sometimes it's permanent, sometimes they end up married."

Silence. The wind blew. The fan swished. And I was sure I must have distant genetic traces of mouse in my family history. I'd have scurried under the desk given half a chance.

"Sounds like rape." He picked up a pen and rotated it like a propeller through his fingers while giving me a dead-set black look. Nerves? Had I unsettled him? "How is that performance art? What exactly do you plan to do?"

"Ah. Yes. Crucial point. I plan to have myself mock-captured, but in as real a way as possible. No sex, of course, but I want to show the changes that might occur in a captive subjected to this sort of situation." I swallowed and imagined shooting all the butterflies in my chest with a dart gun loaded with valium. "I'm aiming to allow a bit of the reality to leak into the situation, but not too much. Women buy stories like this by the millions, so there has to be a mar –"

"No. You are not doing this." He stamped the words out like a man squashing cockroaches under his boot.

I leaned away until the chair hit my back and I could go no farther, then I stiffened and leaned forward again to show he hadn't scared me. "Sorry?"

"There is no way you are allowing a man to do this."

"Ah. Ah-huh. Mmm." Quailing, but trying not to show it, and to give myself a break from the confronting wrinkles on his forehead which pretty much said, *you're one crazy muthafucka*, I reached into the canvas bag on my lap, pulled out my old eReader and tossed it at him. It spun to a halt hanging partly over the edge of the desk just where his lap would be.

His mouth turned down and those sandy-colored eyebrows went a tad higher.

"There. I left a few on there for you to…" I sucked my cheek onto my teeth for a second, "…to study."

Just imagining Klaus reading those stories, some of which I had merrily masturbated to while reading, made my cheeks heat up. Gah, woman. Get this over with.

He tapped the surface of the eReader with his forefinger, like it maybe contained something suspicious. Which it did if you counted the fading traces of hundreds of explicit erotic romances and BDSM stories and…yeah, um, those. The bondage and fucking and humiliating scenes I'd read had probably scarred my brain. It was a wonder I hadn't worn out my clitoris.

"Why should I study this?"

"Because you're the man I had in mind."

Yes. That had gone down so well.

Those stories had made me wonder about the difference between fiction and reality. I'd imagined scenarios, with me in them. Most times the man in my imagination was anonymous but once or twice, he'd been Klaus.

Yes, that day in his office had been so wonderful. I focused back on the present. Klaus was still being stubborn and hadn't signed – nothing new for him. We both had a streak of stubborn, I guess. It had made for some fiery arguments.

Seagulls cruised on the winds, kids ran about laughing on the beach below, but at our table the tension was making my head throb.

"If I sign this you are giving me carte blanche –" He frowned. "– to make you a captive in your home up there on the hill. No neighbors. No contact but me for four weeks." The corner of his mouth twisted. Oh noes – I was in for one of his bursts of silliness. He leaned in and whispered conspiratorially, "I will have you washing my dishes naked in a week."

"God." I groaned. The fucking dishes. That had driven me crazy when we were together. "Klaus, the nakedness is a no-no. You are the one who made me put it in the contract. But no dishes either." No sex, of course, even though I hoped otherwise. No nakedness. No physical damage. His face was to be blurred out. A copy of what we were doing was in a deposit box at the bank. Neither of us wanted Klaus arrested if something weird happened – like the cops showing up.

But needing money was one thing. Washing the dishes was another.

"No dishes, Jodie?" He shrugged. "A bad bargain. Slaves should do dishes."

I raised my eyes to the underside of the mango-colored beach umbrella and prayed for deliverance. Of all my friends and acquaintances, Klaus was the only one I could ask to do this. The only one I trusted to do this. Still, he was being a bastard. While he waited for me to reply, with one finger he slowly turned his shiny stainless steel pen around and around on the table.

I'd never ever done dishes for him. I detested housework to the core. A dishwasher I could load, sure. Hand washing, carrying meals out to a man at a BBQ – all those womanly chores made me shudder. I liked my equality. Women weren't slaves. My fantasies only went so far.

I pursed my lips and sipped more frappe. The bastard abandoned his pen and sat back, watching me with those green-gray eyes. This was ridiculous. After all the mucking around, after days of bargaining, it came down to dishes? He'd helped me with some of the house alterations even. Would he give in if I stood my ground?

"Klaus…"

"Mmm?"

Fuck. As my accountant, he knew I needed money, yet he'd just about sent me to a psychologist when I suggested this. He'd told me that of all my performance art, this was the most extreme. Maybe he was right. No, he *was* right. But his protests and the precautions he'd demanded, the contract with six million sections…before all that I'd been wary myself of going ahead. After I'd had to drag the man to the bargaining table, despite me offering him a share in any profits from the film, *drag, drag, drrraaaag* to the bargaining table, then, and only then, I knew I could trust him.

If filming a woman enacting a capture fantasy and exploring the psychological changes didn't win me a world-wide media contract, I'd eat the damn beach umbrella, with a bucket of beach sand to wash it down. And if I was wrong, I'd have no money for food, and sand would look tasty.

That Klaus had agreed though – that gave me more hope than I'd had for a while. The man only ever bet on near certainties. If he thought this could make money, it would.

He hadn't budged. While I'd run through the encyclopedia of my worries, filed them alphabetically, and then set them alight, he'd barely shifted an inch. His hands lay loosely on his trouser-clad upper thighs. From the corners of my eyes, I dwelled on one of his best aspects. The heaviness of his thighs was all muscle. Being a black belt in judo since his twenties meant Klaus had the musculature of a very fit man despite being almost forty. They'd felt good between my legs when we'd made love.

Thoughts out of the gutter. "Fine." I closed my eyes and shook my head in mock despair. "But I'm not guaranteeing I will. If you can get me to do the dishes it'll be a mind-fuck of Olympic proportions."

"I haf my ways, fraulein."

I groaned. That mock German accent drove me nuts too. Almost as much as the dishes idea. Then he signed the contract, finally.

Relief swept me like a cool breeze, only it sank farther and chilled my bones just a little. Done it. But…yeah, there were limits and rules, but still this was the weirdest thing I'd ever done. And the strange little look he'd given me after I'd agreed to do the dishes had jarred me.

Jeez. The dishes?

Really, if he'd unwrapped an array of knives I should worry. Maybe it was just that he'd gotten me to say yes to something I'd hated so. But I needed a man with some dominance or this whole exercise would have wilted. This needed to have some realness.

As Klaus went to pay for our meal, I brushed aside some strands of hair from my forehead and took a deep breath of the salty air.

In a minute, I was going to climb into his car and drive home, and give him the key to my house. Yes, I must be insane. But if it made me money I didn't care. There was also that niggling other reason. Klaus was hot, like hot in the I-still-dream-of-you-and-want-to-fuck-you way, and that was going to make this even more interesting than it would have been with any other man. Some of his rules…I prayed they'd get broken.

☙ *Chapter Two* ❧

Klaus

I didn't speak on the drive up to Jodie's house. After a few light-hearted jokes that we both laughed at, she went quiet too. The road was dirt and rough, and the gravel sounded like a small war under the tires of my jeep.

I guess we both were preoccupied. Considering what we were doing, I wasn't surprised. The canopy of over-arching gums cut much of the sun as it slanted in over the sea. A glance across at Jodie revealed dappled light slipping over the curves of her face. Her auburn hair streamed backward and bared her neck. She was a beautiful woman. Desirable, but too complicated for me.

Every time I'd seen her up on stage, in the days when I used to go watch her, I'd cringed at the things she'd revealed. It had been like seeing someone trot out their soul on a plate and hold it up for the audience to laugh at. Once, and once only, she'd made a joke of something we'd shared. She'd stopped when I'd made us off limits, but it was too late for me; it had soured things. I couldn't understand her. Willing to do that for strangers and yet she had this thing about holding back with me. Not doing dishes? What was that?

To me, giving of yourself should be more for those you loved, not less.

Was she a good comedienne? From the laughter, she succeeded most of the time, but I knew she'd never make it big. Something about her left her timing a flinch, a half-step, a gesture just shy of perfect.

I slotted the jeep into the space beside her yellow Suzuki Swift and we walked to the front door. As always, her smallness made my manners struggle to break out. I wanted to put my hand on her back and guide her, but didn't. After all, I was to be her captor. This was so odd.

At the door, I held out my hand for the key.

"This is it, huh?" She quirked an eyebrow but tossed her keys in an arc so I had to catch them out of mid-air. "Don't forget the caviar on toast every morning and the champagne on Sundays."

"More like bread and water and cornflakes," I drawled as I pushed open the door.

"Cornflakes?" She chuckled. "Guess I'm in heaven then."

This was a nice little beach house, white with Mediterranean blue trim, a prim delusion of grandeur, a surface coating of prettiness, and buried in the basement, a prison cell. Damn, we were both crazy.

"Down to the bowels of the house, we merrily go," she sang, skipping down the hallway ahead of me.

I smiled and watched her ass. Of the two of us, she was a little crazier.

At least her, I understood – money needs and sexual fantasies.

Me? I didn't need the money. I could do with more, don't mistake me, but I didn't need it. Sexual fantasies too? There was no sex involved though, just the odd feeling that doing this would be...intriguing. Plain and simple, I was curious. At nearly forty, I had an inkling there must be more to life. I felt stagnant and this certainly confirmed that Jodie had a knack of finding things I'd never dream up on my own to do.

And yeah, admit it, man, Jodie still had this thing going. Attraction. I couldn't pass up a chance to be around her. It wasn't purely sexual either. Pheromones? Some special sort of catnip that zeroed in on me? Who the hell knew? I never wanted to see her hurt, even when she was the one hurting herself. Or if I was the one she roped in to do the hurting by proxy? So what was I doing? A psychologist would have a field day with me.

When I got to the downstairs room, she was slowly turning in a circle with her arms out like this was some ballet show, and smirking. "Here it is."

"Yep."

"Here" was a room she'd used for storage, with a toilet and shower attached. The small window up near the ceiling already had burglar-proof bars but we'd put a shutter on also and padlocked it. By the time I'd fished the wrist cuffs from the box on the single wooden chair, Jodie had calmed. I wrapped the cuffs on her wrists, checking out her widened eyes as I did so. There were little padlocks for the buckles and I clicked them into place. New leather smells good, and I took my time, running my fingertip along the raw cut edge before I released her wrists. The look of the black on her white skin said…screamed, vulnerability.

"Scared?" I murmured. I stepped back and waited while she lifted her hands and gave the cuffs a small puzzled look – as if she'd never seen them before.

"Of you? Ha." She bit her lip and audibly sucked in air. "Nooo. Excited, maybe. There's butterflies in here." She laid her palm on her stomach. "I can't believe we are going through with this."

"Me neither. But, if we're doing this, we do it as planned. Even the Fire Department would be upset over this arrangement." I waved at the blocked window. "Let alone the cops. There's no point in going halfway. This film has to be good or we're wasting our time."

"Yes."

I sat in the chair and took the laminated list from the box. I held it up as if checking the words but instead sneaked looks over the top. Her little denim shorts showed a hint of butt cheek when she knelt to sit on the mattress. Damn, what was with me? Peeking at a woman…a thought hit me…a woman who, in a few minutes, I was going to lock inside this room.

For a second or two, I couldn't have blinked if my life depended on it. I stared at nothing.

What was wrong with me?

Was that frisson sexual? I didn't dream of locking up women. I certainly wasn't planning on raping her. I could have sex with Jodie if I wanted to. She'd given enough hints since I broke up with her. But here I was, dissecting her every move.

I snapped my gaze back to the list. The words blurred.

Yeah, the mattress on the floor, cuffs, blocked window, and video camera aimed through the hole in the wall all spoke of normal. If someone walked in right now, maybe we could just say we were being kinky, and maybe the contract would get me out of trouble. Sobering, though. I knew I should *not* be doing this, but if I was then it would be done right.

"You ready?" I asked.

She raised her shoulders in a hesitant shrug and grimaced. "Sure."

"Okay."

As I stuck the list to the back of the door, it seemed like I was rearranging my world, like this was something that was of world-wrenching importance. Why?

The rules were as sensible as I could make them. Jodie hadn't understood why I needed them up in plain view when we'd already figured them out. I didn't know either, not really, but it was important. This enactment of hers was making me doubt my own psyche for the first time since I was a teenager.

The Rules.

1. No sexual contact.
2. Filming is not allowed in the bathroom area.
3. No nudity
4. Bondage is allowed.
5. No physical damage to either of us.

I blinked. Number five was why I'd downgraded Jodie's initial idea of enacting some sort of struggle and carrying-off routine. Ridiculous. That was asking for someone to be injured.

"Bye." Seated on the mattress, with her arms around the front of her legs, she looked comfortable. Very comfortable.

I just nodded as I pulled the door shut. I didn't say goodbye. She wasn't going anywhere for four weeks. The little window in the solid door had a sliding cover. After one last look, I shut it too. Up above on the wall to my right, the light on the camera blinked green at me.

All set.

The back verandah of her house looked out over the forest toward the sea a hundred feet below. The timber of the rail was warm under the grip of my palms. Wings spread, a sulfur-crested cockatoo sailed across the sky – white against the backdrop of gray-green foliage – a perfect metaphor for freedom.

Here I was, free, and she was back there. This was going to take some getting used to. Funny though, as well as a bit of anxiety, like her, there was almost an excitement, or an anticipation? Perhaps. Foregoing my annual holiday to Fiji might have been a good decision after all.

In the quiet, with only the wind and the sky about me, I dared to turn that question over in my mind again. Why? I think I could see now that there was something sexual. My balls had tightened when I'd locked the door and the observation window, and turned my back on her. I liked knowing she was there and couldn't get out without my say-so. Weird, but understanding your own mind is the key to controlling it. There was no point in ignoring my motivations.

I'd partly said yes to this because I knew her and if I hadn't agreed, she'd have found someone else. That was not going to happen. I shuddered to think what another man would do with a woman tied up in his basement. Not that it was my basement, or that she was tied up. Hypothetically though, it would have happened.

But I was a normal man. I had fantasies. The difference between normal and wrong was in how you acted, in your restraint. When someone cut me off on the road, I might dream of a nuclear missile descending on their car and blowing them to smithereens, but I didn't act. I didn't grab a crowbar and beat them with it. I had fantasies about Jodie. I was avoiding them in a way, still. As yet, I didn't want to let myself see most of them. I could taste them, though, at the periphery. This alone, standing on the edge of an abyss into my deeper psyche, was by itself thrilling.

I'd never really figured out the hold she had on me. For all that Jodie had never cut herself loose from me, I'd done the same. Maybe this would settle things and I could stop this absurd need to rescue her from her disasters? Maybe when she got drunk in a few months' time, I wouldn't be there.

∽ Chapter Three ∼

Jodie

After a day of sitting in the room by myself, I was bored. I'd done my planned daily sit-ups and knee bends, and practiced dance routines, including the Charleston, a dance I'm sure Klaus would think was some queer re-enactment of a chicken going into a frenzy. But now I was bored. This wasn't a mind fuck. This was like the worst holiday ever, where the weather was so disastrous you had to stay in your hotel room and read and watch TV. Only you'd forgotten to pack some books, and the power was out. Okay, bad analogy. I had power. I wrinkled my nose and hugged my knees and stared up at the fluorescent tube. I also had a day of nothing much on film.

Maybe Klaus was planning to bore me to death. When he brought in meals he'd been more taciturn than usual. Which meant he'd said all of three words each time. Next time he came in I'd –

The door opened. Lunch. Chicken Caesar salad would be nice. I jumped to my feet and straightened the bottom of my T-shirt from where it had curled up onto my midriff. Annoyance flickered in me when I saw he'd not even bothered to glance at my bared skin. Was I that unappealing? Once upon a time, we'd had a passion for each other.

I sighed at the plate he carried. Over-cooked steak peeked from between two pieces of bread. Cardboard again. "Damn."

"What?" The plate deposited on the floor, he was already stepping away. He waited with his hands relaxed by his sides.

"What? You know this isn't going to get anyone all excited about my film. This –" I waved my arms in the general direction of the entire room. "Is not good enough! Boring me. Feeding me terrible bland meals. It's…it's dead fucking boring. Okay?"

"Okay." He nodded as he spoke. "And what do you suggest?"

Uncomfortable, I shifted my feet. I had thought about this. "Your list…look the whole point of the capture fantasy is that you take charge."

"My list? And what's on there?" His expression was as dead as that steak. Flat, dead, not giving away a *thing*.

Hmm. Klaus was not that thick. Heat seeped into my cheeks. I knew the list by heart and so must he. We'd pretty much agreed on this already, before this began. For a moment, my tongue refused to move.

"Bondage. Try that. And you've got to get more into the swing of things." I lifted my wrists then shrugged and made a dismissive face, even though the very idea of Klaus tying me up had instantly made way more than my face get hot.

Now, he smiled. "I'll be back. One second." He held up one finger, backed away, then he turned on his heel and reached for the door.

The door closed and locked, and I heard him walk upstairs. Maybe we should have written a script. Ugh. I could imagine Klaus doing his fake German accent while growling at me. *You vill do ze dishes and mop ze floor!* Yes, so scary. Not. I made an exaggerated sad face. *Oh boy.*

But bondage was the only thing specifically positive on that list. All the rest were no-nos. He'd deliberately waited for me to say it, hadn't he? Was that his version of a mind-twisting dilemma? I sighed. This was so not working. And he thought he'd have me doing the dishes. Damn. The hot chef from the Thai restaurant would have been a better deal.

Realistically, my other male friends were either wimpy or too odd or not into women. Andrew, for one, was so gay the flowers burst into bloom when he wandered by. Klaus had once held me down on the bed, so I knew he had a little spirit even if he was an accountant. That he'd let go immediately when I protested was good though. And he'd rescued me more than once from a drunken state at a party, dusted me off, taken me home, and been a perfect gentleman. This was after we were no longer a couple too. He'd even fended off one stupid admirer who'd threatened me.

Once, I was pretty sure, I'd thrown up in his car. So, extra Samaritan points for taking pity on a pissed-out-of-her-skull ex-girlfriend. Yet he'd been the one who ended our girlfriend, boyfriend thing. Extra, *extra* points for helping a girlfriend you'd dumped.

I'd never quite figured out what had made us unclick. You know that moment when you click? Well we'd done the opposite. And yet as stark as a photograph made larger than life, I would never forget how gentle he'd been the few times I'd been ill. How caring. Maybe he had some nurturing babying thing going? It was a bit like the Holy Grail of womankind – finding a man who'd bring you an aspirin and mop your forehead. But it wasn't what I needed here.

When the door opened again, Klaus carried a coil of blue rope. Soft rope, I discovered when it brushed against my skin as he threaded it through the D-rings on the cuffs. He hadn't said anything or asked permission, he'd just done it. I liked that. Now this was getting somewhere.

As he towed me over beneath the O-ring that was screwed into the low ceiling beam, a confusing mix of emotions ran through me. The beams were maybe three feet above my head. I couldn't reach them without a ladder but Klaus could. He poked the end of the rope through then led the rope to the side where another ring was attached to the wall. Slowly my arms were pulled upwards.

I'd read this enough times in books to wonder how I'd feel if it ever happened. Embarrassment vied with arousal, but was that me or the books? Was there a difference?

The rope kept moving. Klaus kept tightening it, pulling more through the wall ring, watching me. We'd set these rings up for this very purpose – for some sort of bondage. Still, I felt the urge to distract. My arms were almost at full stretch. "When are you stop –"

"Shh." When I opened my mouth again, he added, "You want this to be your fantasy. Pretend it's something you have no control over. And be quiet."

I nearly choked. Had that been an order? No. No. He was just advising me. He was right though. I closed my mouth. The rope tightened some more and I went up on the balls of my feet. Bursting to tell him he'd gone far enough, I opened my mouth again, and he stopped and carefully tied the rope off.

Klaus folded his arms and leaned back against the wall. Face still, he studied me with those gray eyes.

I stared back and resisted licking my lips, or thinking about how my clit was throbbing, or anything at all of any sexual nature. I wanted him in my bed, making love to me, maybe even tying me up, but now he'd done it, I felt like a display in a shop window. Being helpless while he watched me did something odd to my insides. Like if I gave in, just let myself go, something would happen.

He wouldn't *do* anything though. This was fake. Now that I was here, tied up, I could see it. A man with guts, true dominance…for this to affect me, I needed him, that imaginary man, not Klaus.

I discovered I couldn't relax down onto my feet without the cuffs cutting into my wrists. Minutes passed. My feet ached and I flexed and teetered on my toes trying to get some relief.

"Klaus," I whispered.

"Shh." He put his finger to his lips. "No."

Another few minutes passed. The ache became excruciating, my toe muscles cramped. Gasping I dropped an inch down onto my feet. A minute later my fingers were numb and the skin of my hands was going darker than seemed healthy.

Any arousal had gone south for the winter, but wasn't this what I wanted on film? I struggled to stay silent at the same time as I alternated between resting my feet or my hands. At last I gave in.

I sobbed. "Klaus! Enough. My hands." I looked pointedly at them. "I'm scared they aren't getting enough blood. And this is hurting!"

"It's predicament bondage." He straightened and began untying the rope from the wall.

Oh God. I could stand on the flats of my feet again. Pins and needles shot into my hands. Still bound, gritting my teeth, I eyed him as he proceeded to undo all the ropes and finally reached my wrists and undid the rope from them also.

"You've heard of it?" As he asked, he held my hands and manipulated each finger, then he let go and stepped away.

"Yes," I hissed and shook my hands madly as another bout of pins and needles struck. "Where did you learn about it?"

"The internet. It was interesting. I figured I should do some research so I looked it up last night."

He'd looked it up? Somehow I'd thought he'd read it in one of my stories. Only it had hurt. *Fuck.* Did I want this?

As if he'd read my mind, he spoke. "Still want to keep doing this?"

Good question. I examined my hands again. I was okay. Maybe Klaus had the right mind for this after all. Chickening out seemed silly. The black spot where the camera lens poked through the wall seemed to accuse me of cowardice. "Sure. Sure I do."

He nodded. "Good."

Suspicious, I checked him out. Though he'd always been a man who kept his feelings close to his chest, the lack of emotion showing on his face was distinctly new.

～ *Chapter Four* ～

Klaus

That had been the truth – I had looked up bondage with Google. Weeks ago, I'd also looked through a few kinky shops and blogs. When she first told me about this capture fantasy plan, I'd recognized that BDSM was a close match. Some offshoots of it were devoted to a sort of slavery.

My research had driven me to buy some kinky items online. I'd been curious. Handling the gags had been eye-opening. I knew people used gags, but actually feeling the leather and the weight in my hands, imagining myself buckling one on Jodie...I'd been both fascinated and repulsed. I'd put those into her box of perversion along with the cuffs. Ever since, they'd preyed on my mind like some object in a video game highlighted in glowing red.

Last night the trail of articles on the net had led me from site to fascinating site. I'd learned about a lot more than predicament bondage. I'd joined a site called Fetlife which seemed to have half the world's kinky population on it. By the time I'd shut down the laptop, it'd been four in the morning. Of course, no site had a how-to section on running a "real" capture fantasy. It had all been BDSM, which was consensual. What we were planning was not, or not exactly.

Messing with Jodie's mind would take a little more thought. This was like doing a jigsaw puzzle in the dark using chopsticks. Which reminded me, my God, there'd been some curious things done with chopsticks and rubber bands to women's nipples.

But all of it, the whole time I'd looked, had made me feel slightly off balance, and wrong.

After grabbing a beer from the fridge, I sat on the couch, propped my feet up on the table, and turned the TV onto the channel with the film footage. I rewound to where she was still tied up, let the image burn into my brain, and shut my eyes.

What was it that grabbed me about that? She looked wonderful all stretched out, hands above, with the ropes and the cuffs. Was it just the curves of her body, or the fact that I'd done that to her? Or was it that she couldn't do a thing about it once I had her there? The not talking had been voluntary, but not the bondage. I could've kept her there all day if I'd wanted to – if I hadn't decided her hands had taken enough punishment.

Yeah it was that. My hard-on was back. I thought about taking care of it but no. There was something wrong about doing that.

I swigged a big mouthful and swallowed. The cold beer sang to me on the way down, and Jodie was in there eating my steak cross rhinoceros-hide sandwich. I frowned.

Another swig, another swallow. I placed the bottle on the coffee table and got up. The Chinese takeout in the oven awaited. In the stack of CDs by her stereo, I found one I'd not heard before, Tarja Turunnen. I slipped in the disc.

As I forked the shrimp chow mein onto my plate, I wondered if Jodie had been aroused by the bondage. Though I'd looked closely I hadn't been sure. Her denim shorts, bra, and T-shirt had concealed her body too well.

With the tines of the fork, I separated out one shrimp and toyed with it, turning it in circles. One naked shrimp. Getting Jodie naked was against the rules, though she'd welcome it if I seduced her. Like the porno and the gazillion BDSM shots on the net, that idea was arousing. But I wasn't here to just fuck her was I? That option, casual sex, had been dismissed long ago. I was missing a piece of the puzzle and could not see what it was. With our talking and arranging we'd figured out the limits of this fantasy shoot. But the whole point of messing with her mind was to reach beyond what she expected. To scare her? I'd done that today. A tiny bit. The way she'd struggled to get comfortable until slowly the pain in her hands and feet had overwhelmed her...

I let out a long breath through my teeth. Even if I lost the video, I'd never forget that.

And yet, I also felt horrified that I'd done that. How could I be both? It drew me and it appalled me all at the same time. Protect and be gentle, but turn me inside out and caveman turned up. I'd been so up-tight, so set in my way of life for so long, that this was like a black-and-white photo turning to color.

I sat for a while, elbow on the kitchen counter, with my fork-holding hand cradling my forehead. Wing it. I didn't know where this would lead me, but if ever there was a time in my life that I needed to just go with the flow, it was now.

I speared the shrimp, smoothly slipping the metal into the succulence, and held it up for examination.

I could do anything to this shrimp, but it was dead. Simple and easy to cut it up, to turn it over... Jodie had given me permission for all this. Really, I could get her to let me make love to her, to let me tie her up. In any BDSM scene, permission was required. But, according to her idea of capture fantasy, surely I had to reach beyond that permission and the rules. My mouth twisted. Did I want to? And the *I* was the important part.

Head down, I stared at the fork. Beyond the rules it would be about me and not her, and this was why I'd been so pedantic about rules.

I shook my head then popped the shrimp into my mouth, enjoying the soft crunch of the flesh and the flavors flooding my tongue. It wasn't as if I was going to become Hannibal Lector if I went farther.

The edge above the abyss was fuzzy. If I wasn't careful, I might do things that pushed this too far, yet she couldn't say were precisely wrong. Would the police see it that way? I was an accountant. I didn't want to break the law.

At the chorus, Tarja's voice powered out of the speakers and her singing reached inside me, captured me. Such a beautiful bringing together of voice, lyrics and music into a singular moment, and I closed my eyes in appreciation of the appeal to that one unique sense – hearing.

I swallowed the shrimp and the taste went away. It wasn't the act of swallowing that made the meal spectacular, it was what came before.

I found a pen in my laptop case and some paper, placed it square on the coffee table and sat on the couch before it, pen poised. I wrote the first words.

New List

Something about writing black lines on white made this spring to life. There was a bulge in my board shorts. My erection pulsed. Yes, I wanted to make love to her … no, to fuck her. I always had. Once, I'd thought I was in love, even. So what was different now? Was I going to do it then dismiss her like a snake shedding old skin afterward?

Yeah. What the fuck was I doing?

Then I held the pen for ages, turning it around and around, almost snapping the plastic shaft in half. I could feel my desire to take this further waiting inside me. So many needs crawled around waiting. I imagined them like patient little black spiders all piled up in the basement of my mind.

"Ha." I shook my head. Like anyone, like everyone, I craved stuff that could never happen. I dreaded the idea of ever letting myself go. The old *Lord of the Flies* book came to mind. Peel off the veneer of civilization and people are unspeakable monsters beneath.

The only list I had in my head wasn't civilized, not at all.

Well this man had a fucking thick veneer.

The camera had kicked back into showing live footage and Jodie had begun to talk. The mic picked up her words from where she stood in the middle of the room.

"I was going to try keep this as a role-playing type of scenario and pretend when I talked like this on camera but that seems silly now."

She frowned and paused as if thinking. "So, some honesty. I'm a little stunned by what Klaus just did."

I sat forward.

Still frowning she looked up, dead on the camera, as if speaking directly to me. "That wasn't what I expected. I was, still am, a bit angry. I didn't feel safe. And yet it also didn't tick any boxes for me in this capture fantasy. This is all…" She shook her head. "I don't know. It's all feeling too pretend. Too made-up. I doubt Klaus can ever convince me otherwise. He's too nice. And really, I don't need a *nice* man for this. This is just, just wrong."

Yeah, I knew what she meant there.

I placed the pen hard on the table like I could stick it down by pressing, and shoved back the couch as I stood. I needed to sort this out.

I picked up the whole box of perverted goodies, went downstairs and unlocked the door to the basement, walked in, and dropped the box on the floor. She was doing push-ups but froze and crawled around into a sitting position with her legs off to one side. Her hair had fallen across half her face and swayed before her eye. It looked sexy, daring, like in there, behind that fringe, was the real her.

Real her, real deep dark uncivilized me.

End this. Because for sure, if you don't, this will end badly. Where had I heard that before?

"Hi." A little crease marked between her eyes. "Klaus, this isn't working."

"What?" We'd both reached the same conclusion?

"I thought maybe this could work, but no. I don't think you have an ounce of mean in you. Unless it's for somebody you're fighting in a judo match. You're nice, but too nice. Maybe we should call this off?"

Nice? Like some rusty machinery starting up, defiance growled to life inside me.

I had an *epiphany*. That light that hits when something comes clear – one of those. I understood what was going wrong. The bondage before – what bullshit. I also understood why I felt an undercurrent of anger. All of this exercise in "capture fantasy" was her toying with me and with the whole concept. This documentary was a mockery.

"I agree. This isn't working."

Pure agreeable statement, but she rocked back slightly before she nodded.

"Nice is bad, Jodie? You want mind fuck. You want mean. You want things you dream about. You have no idea."

Her eyes widened.

"Starting now. The rules are gone. I make my own rules."

"Uh. What? They *were* your rules."

I took down the list from the door and held it, slowly tapping the laminated paper against my leg. "No. They were not."

After unfolding the flaps of the cardboard box, I tucked the list down inside and pulled out the two gags. "Rule one. You don't talk unless I say you can." As her mouth opened, with the buckles trapped in my fingers, I dropped both gags into view, and dangled them. "Talk and I use these."

Like magic, her mouth clicked shut. Now I had her attention. That had worked. I was perhaps as stunned as she looked. She touched her tongue tip to her upper lip as I stood before her, and kept her gaze swinging from the gags to my face. I had a feeling I'd never had a woman so rapt in what I said. Addictive. The pulse of excitement had centered at my groin. Nothing I could do about it. I already knew that looking at women in bondage revved my engine. But I'd never done more than look at pictures.

Now I had an inkling that any situation where I got to hold the reins, *really* hold the reins, was like oxygen to a man in the throes of suffocation. Incredible.

I ran through my epiphany, convincing myself as much as her. Bluntness was called for.

"My conclusions. You asked me to do this because you still want me in your bed. You want me to fuck you." Her gasp, I answered by swinging the ball gag. She uttered no words. "Somewhere in your plans, you hoped. The rules, I made up those in line with what I knew you'd be thinking. You knew I'd not step beyond, or not much.

"This," I swept my arm across, "This room was your idea. Your rules. Lock me up. Make me yours for a while, but not too rough or dangerous because that isn't in my rules." I cocked an eyebrow. "Yes?"

Though she frowned and shook her head I went on. It didn't matter if she deluded herself.

"You imagined some safe little love affair, with some kink on the side? Doesn't work that way. Either you hand over control, or I walk. No documentary. Nod if you agree."

I waited. I could almost hear the clocks ticking.

When she nodded slowly, my heart kicked back in. If it had beaten at all for those last few seconds, I'd been unaware.

"Good. This room is no longer your prison. The house is secure and private enough. You're coming upstairs as long as you behave. I'll install more cameras."

No protests. Good. For a woman who liked having an opinion on everything this was exceptional. I could have walked on a cloud I was so hyper-aware of everything she did. Were her lips fuller, her cheeks flushed, her breathing faster? I thought so, but she didn't know what I intended.

"Let me point out what could have happened if this stupid plan had gone wrong. If you picked a less restrained, a less sensible man. You've given me a hundred filthy dirty ideas about what I could do to you. I never knew what depths my mind could plunge to. Now I do. If anyone was mind fucked so far, it was me. Another man would follow through. You think these gags are bad? This one with the red ball is simple, it just stops you talking." I laid the other, metal-and-leather gag across my palm. "This one is a spider gag. With this in, you can't close your mouth and your mouth can be fucked. Do you have any idea of the things on the internet? Wait." I held up my hand. "I guess you do, from what's in those books you read."

I bent and rested my hands on my knees. Mind fuck. This I could accomplish.

"You want a list? How about the list of things a man could do to you in this situation? I could make you wash my dishes naked with a gag in. I could tie you up, cut your clothes off and just stare at you all day – just because I could. I could make you be a piece of furniture and ignore you. Humiliating? Yes. I could train you to be an anal slut. I could fuck your ass all day long. I could collar you and make you crawl around on the floor like a dog at a convenient height for blow jobs. I could share you with the man down the street, stick needles in your nipples and use them and some string to fasten you to eyebolts in the ceiling. Want to try that one? And at the end of it all, if I was the worst sort of man, I could kill you and bury you out there on the beach." I swung my arm up to point. "Maybe no one would ever find you."

Now she was truly speechless, maybe even scared. Served her right. I watched the little swallows she made for a count of five.

"But I'm not going to. I'm your friend. Remember that, no matter what I do." I smiled one-sided but I'm sure it didn't reach my eyes. The eyes are the mirror to the soul and right then my soul was very dark.

Then I squatted in front of her, a couple of feet away, reached out and ran the tip of my forefinger along her plump bottom lip. "My rules. Open."

A second's hesitation at most. She shivered and her mouth parted. Mind fuck, here we come.

"Good. Jodie." Then I very deliberately held up the spider gag, slipped it between her teeth, pulled her head forward, and held her there while I buckled it. Hair made a great anchor point. I slid my splayed fingers into the roots and tilted her head back then I added a rule.

"Second rule. You do my dishes whenever I say. You wear the spider gag. You don't speak unless I say. But first..." Eyes locked on hers, I advanced one finger into her mouth and stroked her tongue. And she let me.

Had I hypnotized her? She did nothing but stare back. What I wouldn't have given to fuck her mouth right then and there.

∽ Chapter Five ∾

Jodie

I wasn't sure why I'd done that, opened my mouth. It hadn't been in my plan, or in anyone's plan as far as I could tell. When he put his finger inside my mouth, though I didn't move, couldn't move with my hair held, a frisson ran through me, radiating out from my lower stomach. No one had ever done that to me before. Like, just, taken over something so private as the inside of my mouth…touched my tongue as if it was theirs. And it was sexy as hell.

I knelt there while he adjusted the buckle at the back, and attempted to figure out my thoughts.

Despite his anger and accusations, I knew Klaus. He'd never do anything bad. I would trust him to the ends of the earth. But if by some miscalculation he overstepped, I could call this off and he'd do as I asked. So I'd play along. Though for a few seconds, a minute or two, it hadn't seemed to be "play".

I would have loved for this not to be play. God, the thrill that rocked me at the thought he might mean this…but no, I wasn't convinced.

He was right about me wanting him in my bed, or me, in his, would be better, but money was what had started this ball rolling. I mustn't lose sight of that. Going along with this rule-less world Klaus had devised was necessary. Besides, it wasn't fucking, as he called it, I truly wanted. Even in the capture fantasies that I read, it all came down to romance in the end. Tortured, angst-ridden love sometimes, which the hero and heroine had to crawl across broken glass to reach, but love nonetheless. The sex was just the icing on the top.

Once upon a time, I'd thought my hero was Klaus.

"That's good," he said to me after the gag was buckled tighter. I blinked at him, at the piercing intensity in his eyes, and wondered what I looked like. So strange, having my mouth open, feeling the air drying my tongue.

I remembered what he'd said about this gag – if he wanted, he could fuck my mouth. This gag hadn't been in my fantasies. His groin was at mouth level and, clearly, from the shape of his pants, he had an erection. Would he? I wanted him to. I wanted him to make me. Quietly, I squeezed my thighs together.

"Come." He beckoned, indicating the open door. On the way past the cardboard box from which he'd taken the gags, he stopped and fingered the edge of the lid. Then he fished around inside and pulled out what looked like a black collar.

I tried to say, *you don't need that*, but it came out a gurgle. With metal in my mouth speech was difficult. My intended words were what I thought I *should* say. I should protest like any good normal woman would. But in truth the collar was as enticing as the gag. They fascinated me. Kinky equipment always had. I was perversely pleased he'd bought these things, and wanted to use them on me.

"Keep going."

All the way up the stairs, with the timber tapping underfoot from my steps, and thumping from his bigger feet and heavier weight, I wondered if he'd use the collar. Of course, when I got to the kitchen, there was the pile of dishes. Ugh. My revulsion kicked in. Sexual domination, sure. Dishes, housework, even cooking for a man, all these for some weird reason repulsed me.

I waited, breathing slowly, surveying the yucky dishes and cutlery, aware of saliva pooling in my mouth and the bright sunshine beyond the wide window, and the line of the sea's horizon beyond that. I couldn't swallow properly anymore. I itched to take the damn thing off and to swear at him a little. Kinky was good. Doing dishes, no, not good. I put my hand up to the buckle, testing him.

"Do you really want to try me so early, Jodie?" He pointed his chin at the dirty plates. The collar swung lifeless, powerless, from his hand. "Go."

Fuck this. Didn't he know how to be kinky? What was he going to do? Beat me if I didn't comply? Sure he would. Not.

I wanted to be his bed servant not his cleaning lady. A trickle of saliva escaped my mouth and ran to my chin. While glaring into his eyes, I grabbed the buckle.

The kitchen wasn't huge, and he was at one end and I was at the other near the sink. In one menacing step, he arrived an arm's length away. That was it – my anger flipped into, I don't know, some sort of euphoric excitement.

"You don't want to do that, Jodie."

My God, the determination I saw in him – this thin-lipped, narrow-eyed man advancing on little me. This was Klaus. He'd never hurt a fly, well a human, unless by accident.

But, he'd put a gag in my mouth, hadn't he. What were his new rules? Did they include fighting back, saying no?

The buckle was wrapped in my hair and I used both hands to fiddle with it as I backed a step. He wouldn't do anything, would he?

A strange feeling came over me – a suicidal courage that made me wonder if my eyes had lit up. I wanted to push him. I wanted to see what he would do. Was Klaus man, or mouse? Between my legs moistened.

Tricky bastard. He advanced, did some judo move, and grabbed one of my hands. When I let go of the buckle to fend him off, he stuck a leg between mine and tripped me. He took me down to the ground in a smooth pivot that relied half on strength, half on gravity. I knew some judo. I'd practiced with him, years ago. I could even remember the name of one or two moves. Ippon seoi nage. That one had stuck in my memory. Not helpful.

I garbled curses through the gag as I wrestled. I wasn't giving in. Fuck him. In seconds though, he'd fastened me to the floor with an arm at my back. I drooled on the floor and choked more swear words.

"Bad, Jodie. Bad." While keeping me concrete-still, he'd leaned in and said that an inch from my ear.

I shuddered at those intimate words, my muscles sagging as if some magic drug had stripped me of my determination to win. But his grip loosened and I revived. When I was halfway off the floor, with my hands pushing me up, he grabbed me again and held me tight. I could barely breathe.

"Let go," I choked out. Through the gag, the words came out like Swedish said underwater.

But he let me go. Breathing hard, I pushed away again, and yet again, when I propped up on hands and knees, he put me in an armlock and forced me over his lap. Held me.

Fuck. Now I *was* angry. Excitement drained away. I summoned energy and fought him. Desperate, raging, gasping, coughing as I fought his muscled assault. Tooth and fingernail, clawing, I even tried to bite when his arm was under my mouth but the metal of the gag stopped me.

He was strong, too strong. Fastened to him, caged in his steel grip and pinned on hard thighs, I collapsed. My muscles burned and had fucking ran out of *voom*. My chest ached as I sucked in air, but I gathered myself, wriggled with everything left…and nothing. I couldn't move.

"Finished? Done?" His words were growled from somewhere behind my neck. Both my wrists were fastened at my back by his hand, my nose was squashed into the floor and, caught on his lap as I was, I could feel his erection sticking into my belly.

"Uck oo," I managed to slobber out, feeling more spit gather between mouth and the kitchen tile it was jammed against. I blinked stinging sweat from my eyes. The speckled gray of the tile mocked me. I'd helped lay these tiles months ago. My heart pounded, everywhere hurt or stung including my wrists where he trapped them. Everywhere was so damn tired.

"Give in?" he asked.

I coughed and considered.

Without warning his hand slammed into my butt and was followed by more and more hits. After one painful knock onto the tile, I arched my neck to avoid having my lips crushed. This wasn't right. My mind flailed at me. It wasn't *safe*.

He kept hitting, kept slamming his hand down on my ass, jarring my entire body, ramming into my mind the finality of his strength. He didn't ask another question or stop, though I half-screamed, half-grunted at the burn from the blows. Tears ran down my face. The force of him, the strength of him, seemed forever planted in my consciousness. When he did stop, it was a million years past when I needed him to. I subsided, gasping, until again my cheek lay on the cool tiles. Agonizing heat flared in pulsing waves from where he'd struck me. Outrage, regret, pain and a strange sort of arousal all jumbled up inside my head.

With my breaths still rasping staccato from my lungs, and my wrists still clasped in one of his hands, he gently laid his broad palm over one cheek of my backside. Ass up, vulnerable, his hand an inch away from my pussy. The situation avalanched on me and, like a rock melting in the devastating heat of a lava flow, I gave in. My muscles relaxed. My body seemed no longer mine.

"Done?" The question floated for ages.

Nothing would happen until I replied.

Then, like before, he inserted his fingers in my mouth. I did nothing as he moved them in and out, playing with me. With one hand on my butt, one inside my mouth, and me lying exhausted over him, I nodded, my forehead sliding over tile.

Yes, I gave in.

"Good."

His fingers left me.

"Now you will do what I ask, when I ask?"

I hesitated a bare second. My heart thumped, I exhaled. And I nodded. It might not last or be forever, but right then, it was yes.

Later, maybe, my mind whispered, later we can argue. But my God, what he'd done resonated down to my soul. This was Klaus? I thought I knew him, all of him. Now…I wasn't sure I knew me, let alone who he was or what he might do next.

୶ Chapter Six ୶

Klaus

When I let her rise, Jodie stood there looking dazed. My hand stung from what I'd done. The clock on the wall ticked. I'd always thought it too loud. The last few minutes sizzled in my brain. Who was the man who'd done that?

Without taking my eyes off her, I put my hands behind me found the kitchen counter and lifted myself back onto it, then I sat there with my legs dangling and I watched her. I'd hit her so hard. I'd never hit a woman like that. Judo was all safety consciousness and a mild martial art unless you combined it with other more contact orientated ones. With judo, you didn't aim deliberately to hit someone hard enough to bruise and I figured I'd made some on her ass. A lot, probably. I wanted to take her shorts off to look. My dick wished that too. I adjusted my pants.

God, my hand hurt.

I could almost see the effect of that spanking draining from her mind. The mental shock was dying. Tear tracks marked her face.

Total confusion was giving way to *he hit me*, and then to *fuck that hurts*. Lastly I figured that defiance had crawled back in and poked at her, whispering, *you don't have to do this.*

The effects were bouncing around in my head too. There'd been mornings when I'd woken up next to her and simply watched her while she slept. The gentle sounds of her breathing, the pure lines of her face unmarred by worry. She looked serene. Beautiful. Every time

I'd seen her asleep my heart had felt that odd warm tug. Love? Once upon a time I'd thought I'd loved her. Then I didn't know. And then I gave up.

And now I was here.

Drool spilled from her lip onto her shirt. She grabbed a towel. Didn't need to think. I reacted.

"Uh-uh." I wagged a finger, real slow.

She flinched and put the towel down.

The *rush* that hit me then – at being obeyed. *Wow.*

Sheer anger burned in her eyes as a string of drool ran from her chin onto the cloth of her T-shirt. With her hands on hips, I swear I saw her twitch her sweet denim-clad ass. Defiance. I liked it.

The drool. Sexy? No. The round shape of her breasts stretching the shirt was sexy, sexual, alluring. That I could make her wear the gag was not sexy, it was…mind-blowing.

Why? I barely grappled with the reasons myself. I'd delivered hit after hit to her ass. And each one had said mine – this is what *I* can do to you, because you're *mine*, right now, whenever *I* want to. I can do anything. For all my fancy words about being a friend, I was more than that now. I'd let loose some dormant part of me. Some other me. A me that didn't just *allow* me to beat her and make her do things. That me got fucking excited and roared when I did it.

My phone rang. I slipped it from my back pocket, and checked the screen. Don, the secretary at the judo club. If I ignored the call, he'd possibly text me, or possibly not. The man liked hearing a voice at the other end.

"Yes," I answered, knocking my heel on the cupboard below and keeping a keen eye on Jodie as she finally did as I ordered and began to wash the dishes. Some weird-ass guilty reaction warned me she might snatch the phone away and run off to call the police. Not that I thought that…but this was so socially unacceptable. Yet I'm sure my dick had gotten even harder when she picked up that first dish. Damn, I was kinky.

"Will you be down the club this Friday to teach?"

I'd told everyone – friends, acquaintances, my locum at the business – that I was not to be contacted, except Don apparently. My excuse was that I was helping someone with a special project. I'd stayed mysteriously silent about the type of project. I had to cover the possibility that I'd be seen around the island.

I held the phone flat to my ear, struck dumb by the dichotomy between the warm friendliness of his voice, and the well-spanked, gagged woman in front of me. Two different worlds. I volunteered most weeks to coach the beginners, the white and yellow belts, but also sometimes I did groundwork coaching with other black belts. I could hear the thump on the mats down at the hall. Hear the barked commands of the sensei. Smell the dust and the canvas and the freshly washed judogis, then the sweat as the sessions wore on. That was part of my life.

My other life.

My hand was throbbing so her ass must be too. I stared as Jodie washed the last dish then wiped it.

The phone.

"Klaus?"

"No, Don. Sorry. I'm busy for the next few weeks. On holidays, but busy. Ian has the schedule. Check with him, please."

"Sure! No problem. See you when you get back then."

"Yes. For sure." I pressed end, and tucked the phone into my pocket.

Some things, when the opportunity presents, you just have to grab them. So I was grabbing my ex-girlfriend and doing whatever I could, legally, that made my dick hard and my mind inhabit that laser-beam sharp thought-place I'd just discovered. I would learn about this dormant caveman, sadist, whatever…this Him inside me.

I crooked a finger at Jodie. "Still hurt?"

She tried to swallow, nodded, then came forward until barely within reaching distance.

Autumn meant the weather cooled some days. But after our struggle, I was sweating, and I could see the sheen of moisture on her neck and bare legs too. Some of that was dribble.

"Your hand." Again I beckoned. With the utmost reluctance, she raised her hand and placed it in mine.

I ripped a paper towel from the roll on the counter then dabbed at her mouth and neck. Without breaking eye contact, I went farther and wiped down where her cleavage was, but over the stretchy cloth, then I wiped under each breast, pressing up a little so I moved them. She tugged at my grip on her hand but I tightened my hold and she made a little grunting noise, and gave in.

My mouth dried.

"Good girl." Oh, the eyes. I could see a world in there. Jodie had pale blue eyes and no matter what people tell you, the eyes say things words could not. Though only a glimpse, I was certain I'd caught sight of surrender in there. When she blinked and turned her head, I dropped the paper and grasped her mouth with my thumb inside and finger outside.

"Look at me." Yes, the blue in there was fascinating. "You have beautiful eyes, Jodie. I thought I knew you, but I didn't, did I? I'm going to study your eyes, and you. I want to know what's inside your head." I pulled her close and kissed her lips on one side over the gag while I murmured, "I'm going to learn about the rest of you, because we have all the time in the world."

Her gasp told me that had hit home. I'd planted the idea that this could go on longer than the month she'd stipulated. What better mind fuck could there be?

But I had other ideas too.

Then I led her downstairs and locked her in after taking out the gag and telling her to drink. With the gag and the drooling, dehydration was a possibility.

Though I wasn't certain where to go I drove into the main shopping area and did a whirlwind shop through several cheaper stores and a second hand one, and found things that might suit my purpose. I knew her size and I wanted her dressed in something not hers. A white lycra catsuit from the second-hand store was perfect. Slutty. My clothes, my body, said that other Him inside me. Not caveman, I decided. I was so rational about wanting to…I swallowed…hurt her, control her, it made the rest of the world go out of focus.

I got milk, bread, veggies and meat while I was at it. It was a fast shop because I couldn't help worrying over what would happen to her if the house caught fire. Ironic, really. She was the captive but I was equally caught. I couldn't go far with her back there.

On the way back to the car, I jerked and stopped when I went past the little café on the beach. Its main allure was having the beach almost under your toes as you sipped your coffee or frappes.

Valentine's Day, all those years ago… She'd stayed overnight at my apartment and we'd made love that morning then had a swim in the slow-surging waves just below here. With the water still drying on our bodies, we'd sat here with ice tea and gourmet chocolates and told stupid stories. The salt water drying on her body, laughter, all those big smiles. A beautiful woman, and somehow we had *connected* back then.

Until I found out that behind the facade was a woman who didn't know how to give.

The memories of our love bleached away in the hot sun as I walked along the sandy pavement. That was then; this was now.

After parking my jeep in the garage, I detoured to the back yard, found a tree saw, and ventured down the steep slope to the left. The closest neighbor was here, hidden farther below, past a huge grove of wild bamboo. Someone must be cutting it back regularly from the short regrowth.

I'd read all about bamboo, about caning. The page with a naked woman bending over with a cane laid across her ass had seared into my memory. Rattan was better. Old bamboo tended to break and split dangerously but green was flexible. I'd just have to be careful. I selected a few good-looking canes and took them with me, swishing at the air as I went. How would she like this applied to her ass? I'd like it applied to her, but with her naked. Those shorts had to go. There was no point in all this unless she got naked at some stage. My dick throbbed. It agreed with that part of my plan.

Legal. Stay legal I reminded myself. Sort of. Yeah. Like hitting someone with bamboo was so legal.

Actually, it was legal, wasn't it? So long as the other party in some way said yes? Whatever. It was tacitly agreed to as okay between us. And now that I understood my own fantasies a bit better, I could explore them, but within reason.

I swallowed and half-shut my eyes at the electric desire throbbing through me. The anticipation was killing me.

✑ Chapter Seven ✑

Jodie

He'd taken off the gag and told me to drink and say whatever I wanted to say to the camera. Though tempted to yell and kick his shins, I'd not done so. My lips and jaw ached and even stung in parts, and for some reason the longer I couldn't speak, the more the center of my chest had ached too.

Being cautious, I'd asked him what I was allowed to say. The man had a hard hand and, though I might overstep the rules he'd made up, I wanted to know when I was doing it.

Anything, he'd said. Well, shit. I had so much waiting to pour out I was lost when he locked the door. The camera blinked at me while I went and got water. My stomach growled. Right then, I'd have eaten his cardboard steak or even cornflakes with wasabi, but he'd taken the plate away.

Weird. For a second I hid my face in my hands, trying to sort out my thoughts, feelings. I was angry, but part of that was because, at times, I'd been aroused. It seemed *so* wrong. I had asked for this. But it still seemed wrong coming from Klaus. My arguments went round and round and round. I wasn't being logical, was I? The anger was burning me up inside and just would not go away.

Logic could go take a hike.

After stalking up and down and in circles for four or five minutes, I sat gingerly on the floor. My ass still hurt. "Anything", coming up.

Though I'd liked some of what he'd done, my need to show I was no pushover reared its head. Perverse maybe, but I was angry and there were things I needed to set straight.

"This capture fantasy is skating on thin ice right now. You're a turd. You went too far, Klaus. I know I set this up and sort of gave you free rein but that didn't mean I wanted you to make me do your frigging housework, and...and hitting me that hard? I may have fantasized about spanking but I have never said I wanted to be hit like that, like someone driving in nails. Or gagged. Tone it down. I need realism. But that much realism will..."

I stopped. Did I want to threaten him with a law suit? No. It was dumb. Leave it be. State your facts and things will level out. Klaus had always been a sensible man.

"Okay. Day two. This has been, I must admit, an eye-opening day for me in some ways. Changing the rules was a smart idea. Keeps me wondering what you're up to. And I did find being man-handled arousing, which ties in with the normal fantasies of women with respect to these stories. If the spanking had been less forceful I might have enjoyed that too. Odd but true. Perhaps I'm a masochist after all. But I'm not a servant. No more dishes. Oh, and please ensure the camera covers any future activities we engage in. I'll edit for effect later of course."

I went on for a few minutes more before stopping. When I heard the distant crackle of the tires across the driveway, it was strange how apprehensive I felt. I found myself tensing and listening as Klaus climbed the stairs. What was he up to? Takeaway would be nice. Sushi would hit the spot. I ran my hand through my hair and wondered if I should ask him to do my laundry. I had enough changes of underwear and clothes for a week but hadn't thought to discuss laundry with him. If I had to take bets, I'd bet that he'd make me do it. Stuff him. No way.

So how was I going to counter his judo moves if he still tried them after me saying don't? Law suit after all? I wanted to make this documentary but could I stand the possibility of my ass being this sore for the next four weeks?

And that time switcheroo he'd tried on me, implying this might last longer than we'd agreed to – not working. Laughable.

I waited some more. Lunch, my stomach complained, need lunch. I lifted my T-shirt and flattened my hand where the cramp was the worst. Breakfast was long ago. Lunchtime was too.

The door opened. Klaus's expression was neutral, except for the steadfast glitter in his eyes. Damn, when paired with the green bamboo cane and the spider gag in his hand, that *look* said scary with a big S. The shopping bag with the pretty blue seahorse on it, not so much.

"Lunch?" I asked hopefully. "Lobster would be nice."

"All out of lobster. First, I need your clothes. Underwear too. Put on this and hand out what you have on."

Uh. Curious. I stared. "You're doing my laundry?" He didn't answer. But no underwear? Or did he have replacement underwear? Interesting, but he wasn't watching me dress. Still mild-mannered Klaus pretending to be Von Schnitzel from some B-grade Nazi movie.

"No more talking."

I eyed the cane warily. "Been doing some gardening?"

He smiled wryly then grated out, "Go change. That's four by the way. Four words you weren't supposed to say."

Four words? What did that mean? I sucked on my cheek. Should I do this? Mysteries made me nervous.

When I headed for the bathroom, he went to my bag, carried it to the door and put it outside. That wasn't just clothes. I'd have to rescue my toothbrush and other things.

I shut the bathroom door. What was in his bag anyway? I pulled out the white piece of clothing. A thin white lycra catsuit, with the sleeves newly cut off and the legs too. Kinky? Perhaps. It would show all my curves without the underwear. But after one afternoon of wear he'd have to launder it. Denim shorts lasted for days with care. His problem, though.

The cut-off shorts part ended at the curve of my butt. My still red and throbbing butt. *Ouch.* I shrugged. He'd seen me naked once upon a time. But after five seconds with it on, I felt the crotch seam working its way upward into my frickin vagina. Like I needed a lycra inner lining. I wriggled and plucked it out. Panties, *really* need panties with this.

I emerged from the bathroom, trying not to walk like a duck about to lay an egg, and handed over my clothes. "No sexy lingerie?"

"Turn." The gag was ready in his hand. "That's seven."

"Seven?" Why was he counting? I scrambled in my memory. Did he not want me to talk? But I had things he *had* to know. Fuck. Had he heard what I'd said to the camera? "No gag. Didn't you listen to what I said on that, earlier." I jabbed toward the blinking light.

"Turn. Nineteen? I'd stop if I were you." He swished the cane and tapped it on the floor. "Yes, I heard it."

I almost spoke but didn't. No point in risking … my mind stalled as I realized I was worried. I *had* called him a turd. My big mouth. I pointed at the gag and shook my head.

"Turn. You don't get to say what I do. Not anymore."

Fuck. I clicked my teeth and regarded him as I struggled with this concept. I knew he'd taken a step toward being happy using force on me. Always it came back to, do it his way, or give up. I didn't want to give up. Wait. Wait and see. If the point comes that I have to stop things, I will. I turned. The gag was just discomfort. I could handle the twenty minutes he'd had me wear it last time. The cane though, I wasn't sure I could handle that. I'd heard, theoretically, that they hurt like hell. If he dared…

With the gag wriggled in and strapped, I was left wondering how I could say no if he did go too far. Gurgling wasn't that good for communication. There were codes they used with BDSM – dropped plastic toys, clickers. Had Klaus bothered researching that? Prickles of nervousness ran through me.

A blindfold I hadn't noticed was wrapped over my eyes. Late afternoon, and bright daylight streamed through the cracks in the shutters, but everything went dark.

Stay calm. Stay calm.

"Your wrists," he said to my ear. And he took them to my front and linked the cuffs together, led me over and used some rough rope to haul them above my head until I was standing tall.

The tippy-toe pose again. Only this time I couldn't see or speak. With my head back, I swallowed, trying to stave off drooling down my front. I wasn't naked. That was about my one compensation for being helpless, tied up, and unable to do a damn thing if anything began to hurt like last time.

My heartbeat picked up. *Thud thud-thud-thud. Thuditty-thud.*

Calm. I said inside my head. My dumbass heart didn't listen and kept on galloping like it expected to run away into a corner and hide there all by itself. Struck by the ridiculousness, I giggled. I was pretty sure that would be gory and fatal.

Do not let him fool you. This is Klaus. Friendly Klaus. Trustworthy Klaus.

"One." I heard him say in a matter-of-fact tone.

Fuck. He is *hitting me.*

The whistle warned me it was coming. I tensed on my toes, rose up. *Thwack.* Fire cut my ass. I jerked and screamed once, then danced in a little useless toe-circle on a one-foot-fucking area of floor while whining through the gag. *Holy fuck! Crap!* After a while I managed to breathe slower. There were nineteen of these? It hurt so goddamned much. On top of the residual pain from the spanking, he'd striped a line of acid.

"Two."

I shook my head madly. *No, no, no!*

Air whistled – the cane travelling away. It would return. I tensed, curled my toes, and tried to will my butt into another dimension.

☙ *Chapter Eight* ❧

Klaus

The next four strokes to her ass made her scream squeakily one more time, then choke out a whole row of little gasps and whines to the accompanying jerks of her stretched-out body. I watched her as she tried to get away. My grip on the cane trembled. Five. I'd hit her quite brutally. Deliberately so. An unholy need to see what this plain-looking stick could do to a woman had reared up and grabbed me. And wow, just fucking wow. Even if I never gave in to the temptation again, now I knew. I absorbed her pain as though it were the finest vintage wine. The camera was there too, with me. But that recording was not the same as this gut memory of her response.

She'd asked me to do this. Always, I kept that to the front of my mind. Not precisely this, but it was necessary for the charade. Though I knew that a part of me was also stunned at how easily I'd slipped into wanting to do this for other reasons.

I was too nice? Her earlier words resonated. Now she knew better. This was me as Mr. Not-so-nice.

I stared at her. My victim.

I'd thought of this me as a cave man. But no, this was more like a monster me.

Did every man have some version of a monster inside him, deep down? Maybe we just needed the right circumstances to set it loose?

I rolled my shoulders to work away the tension. I just had to remember where my monster hid so I could shoo it back into that place in my head when the time came.

Desire rekindled.

Walking softly, I went to her and ever so quietly put my palm on the curve of her ass, soothing her with sounds as I caressed her. Her gasps petered out. She swung her head and stared blindly and shook her head forcefully.

I breathed out slowly as I thought of my answer.

"No, Jodie. You don't get to say when I stop. This pain is teaching you. Take it. Let it pass and remember next time, not to speak unless I say you can. Okay?" I drew the tip of the cane up the back of her thigh, stopping at the crease of thigh and butt. "Okay?"

After a pause, she nodded.

I closed my eyes. *Yes. Another milestone.*

I had to see the damage my strokes had made. With her struggles, the catsuit had rucked up higher onto her butt. The very hint of a red line peeked from under the cut cloth. My dick stood up and hardened as I examined her. I knelt behind her and inched first one side of the white fabric up to the highest curve where it would stick, all bunched up, then I did the other side, smiling at the red lines this revealed.

Her skin quivered and she croaked out, "Mm mmh!" through the gag.

"Was that a no? No noes, remember?" I leaned in and bit her once, delicately, over a line, and tasted salty sweat. Expecting a gasp of pain, I was surprised at the almost inaudible moan she let out. Arousal? I wasn't going to touch her sexually. No, she would have to do that, but...

I went to the rope where I'd tied it at the wall and lowered her hands a little. Then I forced her thighs apart and bit along another cane line – one that was already a darkening bruise. Her whimpers and moans were a pretty symphony. This time, I bent down and looked along the seam of her sex. The cloth had rolled into a very moist, half inch wide section that had worked up into her cleft.

"I can smell you, sweetheart. See you down here. And I see you like the cane at least a little, maybe a lot." To close in and lick her was so tempting I could taste her on my tongue from these few inches away. As I slowly raked my nails down her hurt butt, I exhaled warm air over her pussy. She clenched there and her thighs tensed, but she said nothing.

Concealing her reaction? It didn't matter. She liked this...or something about it. Maybe not all the pain, but some.

I rose. Then I delivered another fifteen strokes at varying strengths, mostly lighter. The last two made her scream past the gag.

Fuck. I wanted to screw her. But no. Not yet. I wanted to make her ask me to fuck her, and I figured she didn't like pain all that much, not yet. So getting her to beg while in pain would be the best result, ever. I could picture her doing it. I was going to make that come true.

I let her down, but kept her wrists linked and I massaged her arms and her legs while she stood there and shook.

But she didn't speak. Not one word. Her obedience was amazing – so good, and after only two of my improvised lessons.

As I kissed and tasted the tears that had leaked from under the blindfold, I said in a harsh whisper, "I enjoyed seeing you scream and try to escape, *loved* seeing you dancing away from the cane. Your ass – I'd declare it a work of art. Yeah..." I touched our foreheads together and looked down over her face, stared into her blindfolded eyes, and at her trembling full lips and those amazing tears. I traced my finger down the wet track on one cheek.

My murmur was soft but as deadly, I hoped, as a knife thrust. "I never thought I'd say this, but I enjoy this. You might be in trouble."

Truth and mind fuck rolled into one scorching bundle. Yes, she was in trouble, but then so was I.

I wanted to do it again. I'd saved her and cared for her so many times. She was a beautiful woman, with a mostly beautiful heart, and I wanted to hurt her and swallow those screams. God, I was so fucked up.

I removed the gag and gave her water, took her to the toilet and waited for her outside the door. Then I cuffed her hands again, sat her down on her mattress with the drink bottle, and gave her five minutes to talk to the camera. From her shifting about and the occasional hiss she made, her backside was stinging. Not surprising.

"Don't touch the blindfold," I said, backing out the door. "Drink some more, if you want to, or talk. That's all."

With the euphoria dying away, I sat on the couch upstairs with the TV screen showing the live camera footage. I watched her and I prayed she would say stop, and I prayed she wouldn't. She didn't say a single word. A few times she glanced up at the camera or above her and her mouth moved as if she would speak but, after a while, she just sat and stared at the floor between her legs. And she didn't touch the blindfold. At the end of the five minutes, I looked at the circles of red where my nails had cut into my palms.

There'd been a time at the judo club when she'd shifted a ladder aside and a hammer some idiot had left on the top had hit her head. I'd seen her fall, unconscious. Praying she was okay, I'd rushed her to the nearby ambulance then followed when they'd taken her to the local doctor. Though she regained consciousness, she'd been sent to the mainland hospital for scans and tests. I'd stayed with her, taken half the next day off work so I could be with her and make sure she was okay.

What the hell was I doing?

She hadn't spoken, but if she had, what would I have done? If she'd said, no more, would I have stopped?

I ran my fingers through my hair. This was how far I'd let this fantasy warp my imagination. That I even asked myself this was ridiculous. The answer had to be yes. Had to be.

☙ Chapter Nine ❧

Jodie

There are times in your life when you feel yourself going in a different direction from where you planned to, and you resist, because change is weird and scary. Same ol' same ol' is calming. But always, there is the what-if factor. So here I was. I'd set this in motion but now I wasn't sure how far to go. Most of all, I wasn't sure how far Klaus meant to go.

It was black behind that blindfold but I'd never been frightened of the dark. If anything it settled me, but I wasn't exactly calm either. I picked at my nails while I thought.

Angry, I was so angry! The pain had made me want to spit on him, to chew him out and tell him how this was not what I'd wanted. With a deep exhale I rocked my head back, looking up at the ceiling I couldn't see. Why? Why had he done that? Did he truly enjoy it? Or was that a lie to mess with me?

Yeah, it scared me if he liked that. Truth be told, I'd wanted sex with him. Rough sex – shoved against the wall, hair-grabbing sex with lots of moaning and humping. But not getting whacked by a fucking piece of bamboo. Shit. Gingerly, I probed one raw line on my lower butt.

How was this fun? It wasn't. Reality hadn't been anything like what happened in the stories.

Sex with Klaus was not on my agenda anymore. Not until he apologized for going too far.

The camera footage would be great, though. I could see how that would have viewers oohing and ahhing. Always find the bright side.

I needed to set a chickening-out point. Past that, if things were going haywire, I should stop everything. Damn and fuck it all though. Already, the pain he was willing to inflict had gone way past what I thought necessary. And yet, when I remembered...my clitoris, that all-knowing judge of everything sexual concerning me, Jodie Partinger, was remembering how aroused I'd been when he'd hit me with that bamboo cane. While I'd been tied, helpless and blindfolded; while I could do nothing to stop him, he'd hit me.

That had got to me. It had hurt, but also it had somehow, just for a few minutes, felt good. When he'd gone behind me and looked at my ass, I'd plain throbbed. If he'd moved aside the crotch of my clothes and shoved into me, I'd have welcomed it. But the man hadn't. Why? I was sure he'd wanted to from his words and actions. Had his sense of right and wrong stalled him?

I guess, it had seemed like rape. Though whacking me with that cane until I screamed hadn't been that much less illegal.

I swallowed. Chicken point, remember? I thought some more.

Any irreparable damage to me was a no-brainer. That would make me shriek *stop* fast, but by then I'd know I should stop things anyway. Problem was I didn't know what he intended. I rested my chin on the back of my clasped hands. Frustration gripped me. When and what?

Scariness. If I got too scared, that would be it, and I could see Klaus meant to make this scary. I hadn't thought he could do this but he'd found his inner Neanderthal.

My ass and thighs stung. Thorough man. I smiled. He was the epitome of someone who lived by the motto, if you're going to do something, do it well.

I squirmed, trying to find a better way to sit, but it still hurt.

My natural tendency was to defy him. I imagined my fingers removing the blindfold, and then I imagined what he might do. Ugh. No. I relaxed my fidgeting fingers. Not this time. I'd be...good. I'd keep myself happy by thinking of how I'd kick his balls up into his teeth afterward, if I needed to. Judo or no judo.

I wish I had a mirror to see. Blood would have freaked me out, though. I prayed there wasn't any, but my ass and thighs burned like hell.

ഔ Chapter Ten ഔ

Klaus

I went down into the room and squatted in front of her. From the lifting of her head, she knew where I was. Quietly, I leaned in and took off the blindfold.

Big eyes. Beautiful eyes. *Mine*, a voice whispered at the back of my head. There was something about being a man and controlling a woman that was immensely pleasing.

Each time, this got a little easier, being her boss, her dominant as the books called it, but I never forgot how abnormal this situation was.

Be bold.

"I'll leave the gag out, Jodie, so long as you don't speak. Say anything, and for every word..." I paused at the thought of what I was about to say. A throb started in my dick. "Each word means I'll cane you three times."

One word. Three times. How would she like that?

I could tell I would. I wanted to see her jump at the stroke of the cane again. So I taunted her.

"Nothing to say? Don't want to tell me to fuck off?"

Her eyes narrowed. Yet though she inhaled through her teeth and glared at me, she said nothing. Whatever swear words were in her head, stayed there. My soul did a song and dance. *The power.*

Temporary, temporary. Remember?

This is all in the name of the documentary. I'm just doing what needs doing to create this fantasy.

I clung to that. Best excuse, ever.

I'm sure what I did next was the last thing she expected. I led her up those stairs and got her to dry and put away the dishes then sweep the upstairs floor. The irate looks grew darker and more frequent. I decided to leave them be even though they were her way of protesting. Give a little, then show her how trivial this performance of hers was. Let her rise a notch, then I'd pull her down again. What a game. This was like chess with her mind, and the wrong move on her part meant I got to do things I could never do out there in the normal world.

While she worked, I peeled and chopped up a banana, an apple and an orange, put it all into a bowl and poured on fresh yoghurt. From the sounds coming from her stomach and the looks she cast at the fruit, she was hungry.

For a startled second, I thought of telling her that she had to give me a BJ to get food. I was sure I could get her to.

But, I could do better. I wanted to make her beg me to let her come. Then I'd get her to masturbate in front of me. It was in so many of her stories. I wanted it like a thirsty man craves goddamned water. When we'd gone out together, it had been another of her no-nos – masturbating while I watched. Sexy, but I'd never seen her do it. I wasn't certain how I'd make her, but I would.

I let her eat then I cuffed her wrists to her ankles with her lying on the kitchen floor before I went to set up the mattress in the living room. I took a last, leisurely look. Hogtied. Such a promising position. Her body bowed backward and the dark areola of her breasts showed through the white lycra. Without looking I knew her crotch would be bare apart from that thin line of cloth. Maybe wet too. I wondered if she was. Did bondage, being helpless, turn her on? It did me, seeing her like that, but I didn't touch even when she glowered at me.

"Wait there." I smiled and I left her.

When I returned a light cream cat was curled up next to her, purring.

I raised an eyebrow. "Yours?"

Jodie said nothing and only compressed her lips tighter together. In this I saw defiance too. She knew I expected an answer.

"Cat got your tongue? If I ask a direct question, speak. Rule. You get punishment for not answering."

"Not my cat, no." Her voice was croaky, as if already she was getting rusty through lack of practice.

I crouched and gripped her jaw. The liquid shimmer of her eyes drew me. "Whose cat is this then?" I held her tighter, felt the movement of her muscles and bones as she prepared to speak. This too was power. Being able to touch her when I wanted to.

"It's a stray. Turned up weeks ago and comes by for food some days."

I let her go and slowly studied her breasts, the arch of her body. When she huffed indignantly, I smiled and moved on to look at the cat.

The creature was thin but not terribly so. Jodie had always been a sucker for animals. So was I. One of our points of intersection. We had many of those despite the ones where we disagreed. I hated those more, though. How had the cat gotten in? Ah. I spotted the cat flap at the bottom on the kitchen door. New. She didn't do carpentry and a hole had to be cut to place that in the door. All for this stray?

I remembered the day we'd found a litter of kittens under an abandoned wheelbarrow in her garden. Their mother had never returned. I'd fetched a cardboard box. Feral as tigers, the kittens had spit at us when we carried them into the animal refuge. I was more a dog person, but cats were cute.

Jodie stared at me, maybe thinking the same.

The cat drew the *real* back in. It blurred the strange little universe I'd been manufacturing. The universe where I was Jodie's master and could do what I liked.

The black cuffs showed stark against her skin. Like badges of kink. I took in her predicament, made by me, took in the red lines on the backs of her thighs, also made by me. I stirred the cloth with a fingertip, traced one line as it ran up her ass and disappeared up beneath the white catsuit. She whimpered when I pressed on a bruise.

I should let her go. I should. Neither of us knew where we were venturing.

I blinked and centered.

Should. She hadn't said to. I'd wait for that. "Cat food?"

"Let me go?"

For a mind-freezing second I thought she was calling everything off. No. She meant the hogtie straps.

"Uh-uh."

She screwed up one side of her mouth but swung her head toward a cupboard. "There."

Inside, I found a box with tear-open sachets.

The cat tucked in like it was starving – and it probably was. The fish smell permeated the kitchen.

"Name?"

"I call it Baxter. It's a boy."

I gave Baxter a pat, feeling the rumble of a purr vibrating its body even though it barely paused in its eating. "Okay. Fixed one problem. Now you."

"Me?" she squeaked.

Ah. Opportunity arises. I wasn't letting this past me. This would make her think.

"That's one word. I didn't ask a question. Which means three."

"Uh." Her mouth clicked shut and she licked her lips. Frown lines shifted on her forehead.

Fuck yeah. Power.

❧ Chapter Eleven ❧

Jodie

Klaus had his fist in my hair. He'd screwed my hair into a single rope then anchored his hand in it. I could feel twinges of pain from the pull on my scalp. With my hands cuffed at my back, I wasn't going anywhere. I gulped as he raised my head so I could take in the living room.

My dining room table was in the center. Mattress on top, along with pillows, and long black straps tied at the four corners. Loose straps. Like they were meant to attach to me. I swallowed, looked at Klaus out the corner of my eyes. After the caning, and his promise of three more hits, I was wary. The way he'd organized everything, I couldn't ask what he had in mind without more hurt.

Unless I stopped everything. BDSM had safewords. Where was mine, I wanted to ask. But capture fantasies didn't have those. I was stuck in this little weird world. I had loads of questions, but if I stopped things, somehow I doubted he'd start it up again with new rules stated by me. He would not be happy. Not this Klaus. Go with the flow. I had a sore butt, sore pride, but I was still, in a perverted way, curious.

"Move." He pulled me over, head down, by my hair.

A blissful sensation rolled through me. This hair thing, I liked. It sorted some primitive thing from my flesh and made me go, *yes, take me*. He'd done it in the past, but half-heartedly.

My groin warmed. The way the seam of the catsuit rolled across me down there as I walked already had my clit wanting more. Embarrassed, I kept my legs together as much as I could. All the…mess down there meant he'd need to give me something new to wear soon anyway. Thank you for something, hormones. From the moment he'd made me put it on, I'd wanted to exchange this stupid catsuit for something else. Something less slutty.

As he undid the clips at the back and freed my hands, I stood there feeling a bit woozy. All I'd had since breakfast was that fruit. Evening was creeping in, cool and busy with insects. Crickets were starting up their chirrups, and bugs tapped and buzzed against the window screens as they zeroed in on the room lights.

"Up." Klaus indicated the table. "On your back."

Hell no. It looked like some sacrificial table. A bed, I wanted an ordinary bed at the least. Then there was the cane lying on the couch. That, I knew. It scared me as much as a mysterious snake slithering in long grass. And belly up? What did he mean to hit?

I started to back away. But his hand was at my back.

"No. Up."

I shuddered, eyed the cane again.

"That?" He gestured at it then leaned down and said to my ear. "Only three as long as you get up now. Struggle and I'll have you ass up here on the floor, cuffed, and I won't be gentle. Rule. You obey, or I punish you."

Another rule? They'd be coming out his ass soon.

His gray-green observant eyes were no longer my favorite color. I tensed as I ran through all the possibilities.

Run? No. Argue with him? Ugh. No. I let my shoulders slump and I shut my eyes for that last bit of privacy inside my head, the one place he couldn't go.

Despite my reservations there was an attraction for me. Being tied like this would make me vulnerable. That appealed, and I think was a part of why I'd read all those books. In a way, this came closer to what I wanted in a capture fantasy than anything he'd yet done.

Okay. I can do this.

With a chair in place I climbed up and lay on my back. Trying not to show my nervousness, I let him clip the straps to my wrists and ankles, and haul them out, tight, stretching my arms above my head and my legs down and out. My thighs had been pulled open. The grip on my wrists and ankles put me in an X-shape.

God. I breathed a little faster and tried not to think of how helpless I was. He'd arranged it so pillows were under my rear and my back. It made my lower half arch up like… I swallowed, shut my eyes…like I was presenting my pussy for him to look at. My thighs angled down to where he tied my ankles to the other table legs.

Couldn't close my legs, couldn't get away, and he could do what he liked. Yet my whole body ached for this man to touch me. The see-through clothes left me nearly as exposed as naked and I couldn't stop panting. I tensed my ass, then did a little squirm on the spot as unobtrusively as I could. I kept my eyes closed. If he saw my eyes he'd know this was getting to me. To be so aroused and so open, yes, I was embarrassed.

There was no camera, or none that I'd noticed. Whatever happened next, I doubted it would be something I'd show to anyone.

Was I being stupid? If he truly liked causing pain I could be in for anything. Maybe next week they'd find me in an unmarked grave with a hole where my heart had been?

Trust, it all came back to that. Maybe he was just going to fuck me? That, I could handle. In the old rules sex had been off the agenda but the reality was, I'd hoped he wanted to. Like any woman, I wanted to think myself irresistible to men, but to Klaus in particular. I guess he was kind of my ideal one night stand guy, except I wanted more than one night, didn't I?

Years ago, I'd almost thought I'd loved him, even if something had been missing from our relationship. What was love though? Really? It had all petered out to nothing.

When I opened my eyes and looked at him looking back at me, studying me like some science project, I chilled. It hit me hard. I wasn't sure anymore who Klaus was.

I clenched my hands into fists and rasped out, "What are you going to do?" *To me.* Those last words, I only thought. *Oh shit. I spoke.*

"Whatever I want to." He put his hand on my throat and kissed my jaw. "You smell good, Jodie. That's twenty-one strokes, I think. I lost count."

For an accountant that seemed the ultimate sin – not keeping track of numbers. I giggled despite that threat. Agony, not to be able to say that out loud. His odd expression made me giggle some more.

"Ah. I get it. Bad woman." Then he smiled and the warmth in that smile astounded me.

He drew back and gently wrapped his hand around my wrist. Then he looked at my body like a man with all the time in the world. I was on display, and pain simmered where he'd caned my thighs and my rear. Yet desire arrived in a hot trembling wave.

His hold on my wrist slipped away. He walked around the table, but kept his fingers on me, sliding them soft as moonlight over the catsuit. There was less than a millimeter of cloth between his fingertips and my skin. When he reached the curve of my breast, I was shocked into heightened awareness. As he circled my bellybutton, I parted my lips the smallest distance and half-closed my eyes. When his hand travelled along the crease between my thigh and the triangle of my mons, I sighed and strained not to arch into his touch. For a few agonizing moments he stopped there, standing at the far end while he retraced, up then down, that line … a mere inch from my engorged clitoris. I recalled in vivid detail the occasions when his tongue had played there. I didn't look at him. I just prayed he'd move on.

By the time he returned to the head of the table, but on my right and not my left, I was having trouble staying outwardly calm. I forced my breathing back to normal and focused on a vase of fresh geraniums on the faraway sideboard on the other side of the room. Who had picked those?

The sun was going down, the shadows stretching, and the colors were fading from the room.

"Look at me," Klaus said softly.

The seconds plucked at me, ticking past, and slowly the strength of his words made me turn my head to look up at him. Only I found him at my eye level, resting his chin on his forearm.

"Hello." He stirred the curls of my hair that lay on the mattress. "Capture fantasy. Maybe." Now he touched my lip, venturing in with his finger to play with the line of my teeth.

"Suck."

I hesitated, but then I closed my mouth into a wet circle around his finger and tentatively sucked. The sexuality of this little act sent a signal down below. I swelled. I'm sure some moisture leaked from me. And I couldn't look away. My pussy did one of those tiny spasms telling me precisely what my body wanted. After all he'd done to me, and this, I still wanted him to do dirty things to me. Things no sane person would want.

He withdrew his finger then slowly plunged it back in and out. "I think… I think you're my slave right now, Jodie. Or close to it, in your mind, and in mine. To be honest, nothing we have ever done together has been as amazing as this. I'm in love with making you hurt and wince and scream, but I also want to watch you come. I want to fuck your gorgeous mouth and your ass more than I ever did before. I want you mine more than ever before."

Oh crap. How much was true, how much was mind fuck? I didn't know. From cringing at the pain notions, I'd flown straight into being enthralled. My libido was sitting up and panting with its ass in the air.

"But first I want to see you masturbate in front of me."

Ick. No. Uh-uh. I squirmed inside and my libido ran away and hid.

"You haven't said a single word. That's so fucking good. It pleases me. Never thought this sort of power would get to me. But it does. Another thing," he murmured. "I don't ever want to let you go again."

Everything screeched to a halt. Not let me go? That might be good, or it might be very bad.

"What are you thinking?"

A question. I could speak. I licked my lips, remembering the feel of his finger sliding in. "I'm thinking that ..." The words seemed odd on my tongue. "That you're not that good an actor."

He smiled slightly. "True. I'm not. And?"

And what? "And so what you just said is fucking scary."

"Don't swear."

My throat tightened. Just because he didn't want me to I was worried. The cane, the whole way he'd taken hold of the situation, of me, it all muddled up together. I didn't want to swear. Not with him staring at me like that.

"As soon as you masturbate for me, we can move on."

I wasn't sure I wanted to "move on" anymore. I was confused and horny and scared and so fucked up in my head. At least I could swear in my mind.

Fuck fuck fuckitty fuck.

No, that hadn't helped.

Evening had arrived and it was dark outside. When he switched off all the room lights except for the softer up-lights, the room became an isolated cave. The front windows were open and the louvers rattled in the sea breeze, but no one could see us. I was alone with Klaus. Tied up and alone. I strained at the cuffs until the edge of the leather scraped my skin, twisting my wrists, seeing if I could slip loose an ankle or a wrist. No. Loose but not loose enough. I was unable to stop him doing whatever he had in mind. And that, admit it, that turned me on.

"Done wriggling?"

He smirked at me then went and set up the standing lamp that I used in jewelry making. By screwing back a knob he focused the light down into a small circle on my crotch. I could feel the warmth of the light. I could tell I was very wet down there. I could also tell the catsuit would be concealing almost nothing because it had gathered between my labia.

I was horrified. It had been a warm day and I'd suddenly become sure I needed a shower.

The reflected light on his face showed he was rapt in what he saw. Me. All icky and ugh and I wanted a damn shower, and a change of clothes, and *then* I wanted him to do nasty sexy things. I wasn't doing anything without a shower first.

Again he touched me, massaging my inner thighs and my feet, my legs and my body, but not going over any erogenous areas. So *close* to where I wanted his hands.

If I held my breath, I could imagine his fingers straying sideways, bumping and sliding over the lip of my labia then dipping inside, playing in my moisture. I remembered his fingers from other nights – thick, manly, just right for fucking me. When he shoved two or even three of them inside at once, the stretch on my walls was electric.

I got so wanton I angled my pelvis sideways an inch or two to encourage him. No luck.

I exhaled as quietly as I could, small shuddery breaths while the want pumped in, filling my body to bursting.

God. Touch me already!

But, he teased me, got me aroused, then he went aside and sat on the couch and read a book. A book! I raised my head and glared. After a minute or two, I squirmed once, wishing I could rub my legs together. Another few minutes and I couldn't help squirming some more. I wanted his touch. He kept reading, the pages turning methodically as if I wasn't tied up half-naked on the table.

Bastard. I could see where he was heading with this.

And just the idea of it kept me thinking about coming. I squirmed some more. For half an hour he alternated reading with massages then he went to the kitchen and returned with a jug of water. Ice water that he dripped onto my groin and my breasts until I gasped. At least I was cleaner. Numb in spots, less horny, but cleaner.

To my annoyance he kept up the dripping until I was certain the mattress would be getting soaked. His warm palm touched my thigh and he held me there. He stopped me from dodging the icy coldness with that big hand of his wrapped across my inner thigh muscles. I flinched. The contrast of hot skin, him controlling my leg, and the cold water dripping onto my clit confused my body. I shot straight back into arousal and had to bite back a groan.

The massages and the cold alternated. He remained silent. A moth came in and flew about the lights, battering itself endlessly. I was ready to combust, but I kept myself fairly still and quiet even if now and then I clenched down there. Even if my clit was standing up hard under the cloth. With the light focused on my crotch, I could think of nothing except how much he wanted me to come.

Then he went away again and returned with one of the white candles I kept in reserve for power failures. I squeaked at the flame as it danced in the breeze. Lycra melted didn't it?

"Worried?" He inserted his hand under the cloth above my leg, tented it up. I watched anxiously as he dripped wax onto the cloth over his hand. "Don't be. I know the melting point. I give you permission to scream if it hurts, but if I check and find you lied, I'll punish you."

He hadn't followed through on that last punishment but I wouldn't lie. It wasn't worth the risk.

Rigid, I waited for the first drip as he held the candle above my leg. It hit and heat spread. Bearable. I relaxed as the line of wax advanced up my thigh and only tensed as it neared my groin. I pulled at the cuffs, wriggled my butt a few inches up the pillows to get away until he held me down. I squeaked at the impact. Warm only. The first drips there pattered around my clit. He moved up my body drawing a line toward my breasts. Tap tap tap. My nipples budded tight and poked up like tiny beacons.

"These are mine," he whispered, and his hand gripped the base of my breast. The candle was above me. The pool of wax at its top end glinted when he tilted the candle. I groaned before the droplet hit my areola, as much from his possession of my body as from the promised heat of the wax.

This time I couldn't stop myself arching into the air. From my nipple, the heat flowed to where he held my breast in the half circle of his hand.

"Want something?"

I wet my lips but only stared as he shifted his hand and took hold of my other breast. Then he warmed the tip of that nipple with more drops of wax. Desire trembled up and down my body, rippling, gathering where the wax sent liquid heat into my skin.

When I was panting aloud at each new drop, he blew out the candle and left me in the dark. The wax dried. My need waned and I became aware of the stiff wax crinkling the material. Arousal was there but lessening.

The creak of the couch and the floorboards told me he was coming over. Metal glinted then I heard the distinctive purring snick of scissors opening and closing.

"Interesting. I wondered if you'd beg to come after that."

Not a question. How could I beg without speaking? I guess I'd wriggled enough, though, but I wouldn't give him the satisfaction of thinking I was that malleable. And I couldn't conceive of doing what he wanted. Just the idea of masturbating in front of him made my lady bits shrivel.

"I could try to get the wax off with a knife but I doubt it would work. And so…"

For the first time he touched me directly and intimately. His finger and thumb found one nipple. I had time to squeak once before he tented up the material, brought the scissors close and snipped away a circle. In the half-dark. He'd cut right next to my nipple, in the dark. I shrank and tried to merge with the mattress. Damn. Then he grabbed my other nipple and did it again. Jeez!

When he grasped at my groin I was ready and only caught my lip between my teeth and whimpered. There was light down there. He wouldn't cut any of *me* off. Would he? I held my breath while I listened to the metal blades scissoring shut, as they cut. The pull on the catsuit lessened. Cool air brushed my nipples and clit.

"Better."

I squinted into the light. The coolness there made it clear he had done what I thought he had.

"Want to say anything, Jodie?"

"Why?" I shook my head. "I'm still not doing that and I need a shower, and now I need new clothes." Unless he wanted me to parade around with holes there. But, I guess he did.

"A shower it is. I have to cane you first though."

Crap. He hadn't forgotten? I wanted to stay where I was. Twenty-one was too many by far.

But he unstrapped me. Once I'd climbed down on shaky limbs he linked my wrist cuffs at my back and forced me to my knees, then pushed my head down.

He hissed. "The sight of you there, waiting, is dick-hardening. Twenty-one."

Twenty-one it was. I flinched as each hit burned across me. Not as intense as before, nowhere near it, but enough to make me sob and catch my breath in little gasps. I couldn't lift my forehead from the floor for a few precious seconds.

On the march to the shower, he stopped to feel between my legs. With one hand anchored on my shoulder, and forcing me to bow down, he sent his other hand cruising along my slit. Tingles erupted into my body. I was so wet I could hear the slick sound. My lower lips were extremely swollen – a natural landing strip for cock, or his fingers.

I shuddered and gave in. So unexpected. I hadn't thought he'd do this. Though his fingers stayed outside of me and fire still possessed my rear end, with all the wax and the massages and with my skin naked in just those naughty places, I'd become excruciatingly sensitive. He pulled his fingers back along my slit, brushed gently over my clit, then waited with his other hand still on my shoulder.

I could have screamed with frustration. I was bent over, hands still cuffed at my back, and sucking in breaths though my teeth. My lower body and my bared nipples throbbed with every heartbeat.

"Ready to show me?"

"No." I straightened. "I told you that. I can't."

Klaus nodded. "Okay." Then he recommenced our march.

At the upstairs bathroom he pulled me into the room and got the shower on, then pushed me under the water with my clothes on. He unlinked the wrist cuffs. I'd had the shower redone, tiled beautifully, and it was large enough for two. My ass stung briefly but oh my God it was good. The water sluiced away all the dirtiness, all the craziness of the past few hours. Eyes closed, I reached to undo the front zip.

"No," he growled.

I cracked open my eyelids.

The man had gotten naked and he stepped in with a very nice erection pointing my way.

I grinned. This was more like it.

"No," he repeated. "Don't touch anything. Don't speak. Do not take your clothes off." Then he crowded me with his muscled body until I was pressed up against the tiles with his cock poking into my stomach. The water poured down us both.

I couldn't help moving against him. Inside me, now, I wanted to demand. I groaned. I couldn't say that. The cane kept me silent.

"Good. Quiet is good. Stop humping me."

I stopped, held my breath while we locked eyes.

While he pinned me there, he shoved his hand to my throat and jammed me into the wall even more. I could breathe but couldn't move. With his power demonstrated in every movement, and in every word, he leaned in until his warm breath brushed my ear. "Now you will make yourself come. Now. Not in one minute or one hour or tomorrow. Now. Put your hand between your legs." He gave my neck a shake.

Crap. I was stunned. Before this, he'd beaten me, given orders, done all sorts of things that had aroused me, but this...*this* had tipped me into some new land where Klaus was more than a man, something far more. This was not some role-player, this was *him*, his desires, and his sole aim was to master me. My willpower crumbled beneath his iron-hard stare.

Shaking, I moved my arm. He gave me some distance though his hand stayed at my throat. I squeezed my trembling hand between his stomach and mine, the back of my hand grazing his cock. I slid my hand farther until my fingers reached my clit. That first gentle touch made me exhale sharply. I circled my clit, made it move, and I stirred to life that familiar tide. The pressure that had been building all night slammed back.

"Keep going. Get yourself off. You were so wet down there in the living room. I could have slid inside your cunt in an instant. But I'm waiting. You want me in you?"

God yes. I swallowed, then I nodded the smallest amount.

"Stick one of your fingers up there. Fuck your cunt for five strokes."

I did. I shifted aside the remains of the catsuit where it had jammed up into my pussy. I moaned and panted and pushed my body into each stroke of my finger. The rhythm of an impending climax settled in fast. And he watched. Eyes on mine, on my face, though sometimes he glanced down at what my hand did, and always he held my throat. It was that, I think. Him taking me as his. Him telling me what to do. Hot. Sexually demanding. I pressed at my clit and fucked myself, got myself higher and higher, until the thump in my temples and my groin erupted into the mind-blowing feeling of a full-on orgasm. He put his hand on mine as I arched myself out from the wall and cried in pleasure.

I opened my eyes. His hand was down there still, stopping me from pulling away.

"Yes. You did it for me. Just like I wanted and it was beautiful." Then he bowed his head and kissed me, crushing my mouth. My head thumped into the tiles. I gasped as he forced his tongue inside. My thighs trembled.

"Stay. Stay there."

With no other warning he put his hands under my butt and lifted me up enough so he could slide his cock in. That first probe as the head of his cock found my entrance made my eyes roll back. Rapture poured through me. I was wet like he'd said. Nothing stopped the pump and exquisite glide of his cock. Water poured over us, drowning my whimpers when too forceful a thrust battered my hurt flesh into the wall. My pussy clamped onto him and he hammered in, again, again. I put my hands on the muscles of his shoulders and hung on. I was a woman swept by a storm. Every thrust sank home to the last inch, stretched my inner walls, and slid my back up the tiles. Each stroke wrenched a cry from me.

When he came the warm swell of his cum triggered another ripple of pleasure. I groaned loudly, and slumped, held there only by his body. Used and tired, and everywhere on me either hurt or thrummed with pleasure.

He hadn't put on a condom. I guess he figured I was still on the pill. Maybe he'd seen the packets in my bag. I was on the pill. Luckily. Right then I didn't care about the whys. All I cared about was my new appreciation of Klaus. Scary at times, yes. I had no inkling as to what he would do tomorrow, let alone in the next minute.

I fumbled to understand myself. Humble, overwhelmed, yet I also had a strange sense of belonging. The world was a frightening place and for once I had someone who saw me at my most basic, as who I truly was, and still wanted me.

∽ Chapter Twelve ∽

Klaus

I woke before Jodie and lay on my side watching her breathe. Naked, pretty, and mine. All those curves...I admired her awhile, feeling my dick awaken too. I'd let her come to bed with me because that's what I wanted. I could have made her go downstairs again but having her warm body beside me was far more satisfying. Last night I'd taken off the wrist and ankle cuffs to let them dry and I'd given her some soluble painkiller after watching her grimace when she tried to get comfortable.

This was her bed, of course. The bedroom was pretty and feminine, with a sunny yellow, lime-green, and cream color scheme. In the distance I could hear waves surging up the beach and seagulls crying. Above our heads, the white lace curtains blew like wisps of nothing in the morning breeze.

She faced away from me so I could see the marks I'd left on her skin. Real bruises striped and dotted her butt and thighs in many shades of darkening red and faint blue. They fascinated me and made me think about creating more.

The cane would have to be rested for a few days while she recovered. But there was a crop in the box too. When I'd ordered online, the impact toys and implements of pain had drawn and fascinated me. Jodie might be horrified if she saw them. I planned to try them all in the coming days.

This had changed from some onerous task – helping her do a weird documentary – into an adventure. This was what had been missing from our relationship. All those notions where she'd held herself distant from me – not happening anymore. This was what I needed. Control. My terms. I inhaled deeply. And I wanted this new perverse kink of mine too.

When she stirred, I got up and retrieved the cuffs from the top of the antique chest of drawers as well as the collar I'd put there. My dick hardened as I strode back to the bed.

I knelt beside it. Blearily, she opened her eyes. "Good morning, Jodie."

"Morning," she whispered.

A smile began to form on her lips.

"That wasn't a question." I waited for her response, hoping it would be a good one.

Her eyes flew open.

"One word. Three hits." I stood, slid my arm under her torso, and hauled her from the bed so she sprawled facedown onto the rug.

Though she let loose small, angry screams and struggled like some beast – a cute sexy one – dragged from its burrow, I easily subdued her. I was heavier, stronger, and I could take down a man my size or even larger, if he wasn't good at fighting. Jodie had zero chance.

Straddling her, and sitting with some of my weight on her back, I got both cuffs back on, locked, then I clicked them together. By then she was breathing hard. Her body pushed me upward with each labored breath.

I whacked her once, lightly, on the ass and she squealed and drummed her legs against the floor.

"At least you had the sense not to say more words."

Her petite growl made my heart lift and my lips twisted into a grin. Such a fucking thrill, wrestling her down when she resisted.

"You're getting this on too." I dangled the collar before her eyes.

"Mm-mm!"

"Oh, yes." Then I looped it around her neck, buckled it, and locked it. "All those BDSM freaks like to have collaring ceremonies. "Not me."

I rolled her over so I could see her face, though I didn't use my weight on her much at all, since that would have crushed her arms under her back. Her breasts wobbled and I couldn't resist. I grabbed both her nipples and squeezed until she flashed a cross glare my way. Then I squeezed some more, only letting go when she bucked under me and whimpered.

"This..." I ran my fingers under the collar. "Is staying on. It makes you my little captured slave. Doesn't it?" I cocked an eyebrow.

"No." She bit her lip, then waited with widened eyes, as if afraid she'd gone too far.

"That's okay. I asked you. I disagree, of course. We have weeks, months, years for me to convince you. One day you'll answer, yes. You'll kneel and kiss my feet and say, Klaus, I'm your slave. Hey! Stop scowling."

More mind-fucking fun. Though part of me was ecstatic at the thought of that coming true. I gave her body a jiggle by rocking my thighs. Then, like a king bestowing some great reward, I raised my forefinger and planted it in the center of her forehead. "Not that it matters. If I say you're mine, you're mine."

Alarm flared in her eyes.

I drifted my finger downward until I reached her mouth and I inserted my knuckle between those sweet lips. This time I didn't have to ask. When I waited a while with my finger there, I saw some change come over her. Her body relaxed, her eyes seemed to soften, and she licked me, then she sucked and licked again. Her tongue tip was damp and soft.

Slowly the anxiety in her eyes ebbed and vanished.

I lowered my head, gently kissed beside her ear and whispered, "Good girl."

I would have liked to have fucked her then and there, but I didn't.

I pulled on jeans, aware of her nakedness beside me. We went to the kitchen and I ordered her to make pancakes. Cooking for me, although she'd done it before, I'd always sensed it was with reluctance. For a woman, Jodie had a poor mothering instinct. Not that I wanted mothering exactly. But I figured a partner should want to care for the other.

But this time I had the upper hand. Though getting her to cook naked was bad when something hot might spatter. At my direction, she put on an apron that covered her front but not her ass. So while she cooked, I made sure to play with her tushie now and then. I squeezed it, I fondled it, and in spite of her squeals, I even bit it once. And I dreamed of fucking it. Damn the woman had a nice ass ... a nice bruised ass.

"Now, you're done," I said, when the fry pan stuff was finished with and a pile of pancakes awaited on a plate. "You can sit up here." I patted the counter top to the right of the sink. "Spread your legs and play with yourself."

The look of horror on her face was amazing but she was learning. She compressed her lips.

"That bothers you? Doing it here? After cooking? Good. Get up. Obey and I won't use the cane as your punishment. Take off the apron, though." I advanced and squashed her against the counter while I reached behind her to undo the apron bow. I bent down and gave her a few kisses while I fiddled with the cord and unraveled the knot. Her sighs weren't long in coming.

I kissed her again, drinking in those sighs.

"Good." I pulled away, watching her as I did so. She was so complacent compared to the Jodie I once knew. It was kind of beautiful. If I could keep her this way forever, I would.

I took the apron off over her head, and tossed it aside.

"Up." Again I patted the counter. This time she slid along and carefully hitched herself upward, sat, then spread her legs, ever so slowly.

God damn. That would never get old. All those pink bits on women would never *ever* get old. But…look nonchalant, in command. No, fuck it, not doable. I held back a swallow then stepped away and leaned against the wall with my erection pushing at the zip on the jeans.

"Let the show commence. Play with yourself."

∽ Chapter Thirteen ∾

Jodie

This was not normal. No one sat on a kitchen counter naked and masturbated for a...no, he wasn't a boyfriend. What was he? I stared. Klaus wanted me to say I was his slave, which made him my Master? No way. That was one step too far for this liberated woman, no matter how many erotic books I read.

"Start now," he growled.

I jumped. My hand went to my groin, to my clit. I sucked in a shaky breath at the way my clit had suddenly become the center of *everything* – of his gaze, of my body, of what I was doing. Things awakened, tingled. My finger and thumb down there found that rightful place I recalled from so many nights alone. Only this time Klaus was looking...like last night. The amazing last night. It bothered me, then as I adjusted my thinking, it aroused me more than I thought possible.

I'd done this. I closed my eyes and played. Fingers manipulated and rubbed, thrust up inside me to the sound of liquid squishes. My clit rose higher and welcomed the rhythmic caress of my finger and thumb. I arched, hearing my own ragged breathing, and knew that with a little more I'd be there, gasping in ecstasy.

"Stop."

Incredulous, I opened my eyes.

Klaus shook his finger. "No."

Obedience had become second nature. I withdrew my hand and despite the throbbing in my groin, I waited, still with my groin presented for him.

"Hop off, turn around and lie your front on the counter with your ass out for me to see."

Like most of his recent commands, I could see little if any emotion behind it. Yet I knew he must be aroused. The bulge in his jeans said so. That, got me going. I loved the thought I could do this. I didn't care if he wanted to thrash my rear end and make me scream. I wanted to please him.

Oh fuck. Bad. I'm going down some Alice in Kinkyland rabbit hole here.

I slid off, wriggling as my poor bottom stuck here and there. Then I turned, and lay on the counter, my breasts on the cool top, so I was showing him my ass. I waited. My awfully loud clock on the wall ticked like crazy. I shifted, arched, and presented my ass even higher, knowing what a wanton slut I must look like. That got me even hotter.

"You look so fuckable."

Those words riveted me to the spot. Klaus hardly ever swore.

As his finger toyed with the edge of my entrance, slowly swirling around, stretching me, my eyelids fluttered at the pleasure. Then he stopped.

"This first. To clear the slate."

He struck my ass with his hand, twice. The slaps rang in the little kitchen and left me panting, head on the counter, mouth agape as I huffed hot breaths into the laminate. That, I'd liked. So hot. It hurt but the afterglow had made my whole lower body come alive in the very best way.

I heard the unzip of his jeans.

His cock pressed into my entrance.

I quivered, waited, felt the slow push and slide inside. The slow stretch. Oh God.

"Doing good, Jodie. Do not move."

I didn't. But I groaned as he pushed his cock in, and then out. The shunting movement was so excruciatingly gradual that I wanted to thrust back. But I didn't. I was good. I bit my forearm, and let him do it all. A climax built and built as he kept going, fucking me slowly. He paused, balls deep, so deep I was filled to the brim and gasping, groaning.

"Now, I'm stopping. I'm going to fuck your mouth instead. I'm coming inside your mouth, with your juices on my dick, and you will swallow."

Then he pulled out and was gone.

I keened.

I fucking keened. I wanted him back in. I wiggled my butt, enticing him. One. More. Thrust.

"No." He slapped my butt gently. "Turn. Kneel. Open your mouth."

This, was pushing it. Blow jobs, I could do, but when I wanted him inside me so fiercely? I slumped with my forehead to the laminate. Then I did as he ordered. Exactly. I slipped to my knees.

And I opened my mouth, knowing what he intended. I met his eyes.

"Eyes down, Jodie," he said quietly.

I did it. I let myself just be. I'd never tasted myself but that somehow made this better. I thrilled to the thought of being used.

With his hands on the counter to either side of my head, he thrust into my mouth, slow enough to let me get used to his bulk inside me there. Saliva built, slickening. He almost reached the back of my throat. I coughed, gagged, but he stayed there. I could do this. Had before. I swallowed desperately, eyes watering. Then he began to fuck my mouth in earnest. The rhythmic in and out let me catch my breath just enough. Just. Enough.

"That's. Good," he said huskily.

His thrusts intensified and his cock went in and out faster, harder. At last I felt the thickening and pulse as he came. His hands wrapped in my hair. His cum jetted down my throat. Semen reminded me of bad oysters, but I gulped it down and when he withdrew, I swallowed air, gulped some more.

When he released my hair, I looked upward, pleading with my eyes. *Now, me?*

"No." He shook his head. "Now we eat. Rule. You stay on the floor when you eat."

Crap. He had to be joking.

No. He was not.

* * * *

The plate was in front of me as I kneeled beside his chair. I stared down at it. Klaus ruffled my hair with his hand and passed me the maple syrup. I looked up at him and he gave me a small knowing smile, as if he waited to see what I'd do.

With my palms on my knees, I frowned again at the plate, thinking, trying to decide where I was at.

I was going to do this.

I didn't know what it was about the situation that drew me. But I thought it revolved around belonging to him so deeply that it felt right. It was novel, thrilling and comforting. I could let him turn my ass black and blue, let him fuck me when he wanted and yet still be happy.

This was life brought down to its most primitive elements. Relying on someone else for everything.

For a supposedly pretend thing, this situation was becoming ever more surreal. But also ever more addictive. One day this would end, and where would our relationship be then? Where did I want it to be?

A memory came to me of one Valentine's Day when we'd fed each other strawberries and chocolates down at the café on the beach. I'd threatened to bite his finger, but sucked it instead, in humorous, teasing way. He'd made me laugh that day. I'd never have let him, that *him*, do what Klaus had done to me just now. I'd have chewed him up and spit him out.

When I got angry with him back then, he'd mostly just sit and take it. Sometimes, he'd frown. Sometimes he'd explain why I was wrong, and sometimes he'd end up sulking and not talking to me for a day or two. And that, I realized, had made me despise him, just a little.

If I snapped at him now, even spoke out of turn, he'd have me facedown and caned so quickly. A shiver ran through me, cold and fast. Goosebumps. I stared some more at the floor. God. I liked this new firmness. I did. I must be mad.

Unhurried, I poured some syrup on, gave it back to him, took up the knife and fork, and I began to eat. On the other side of the coin, I was famished. He could have fed me whale blubber outside on the lawn and I would have eventually obeyed him.

When we'd eaten, I reluctantly washed up. Upholding the feminist tradition of self-righteousness and self-reliance was too ingrained for me to feel that doing this for a man, providing for him, was right. It always screwed with my sense of *me*.

The last dish dried, I turned to find Klaus there, crowding me back. By covering both my hands with his and pressing down, he nailed my hands to the counter top to either side. Then he kissed me thoroughly until I was afire again. I angled forward, grinding my hips against him. But no relief was in sight.

"You can come in a few days, if you behave." He lowered his lips to mine and this time, he slipped his knee between my legs. The heavy muscle of his thigh was right where I couldn't escape it. My arms stayed pinned out to the sides, and with my smaller body jammed into the counter by his weight, I could do nothing as he kissed me some more, breathing hotly into my mouth.

This was as restrictive as bondage. As freeing. I stopped struggling and gave in. When he ceased kissing me, I was shaking and my head was bowed back. He let me up and put his finger on my poor assaulted lips then rolled out my bottom lip a little. A familiar place for his finger. I licked him and delicately sucked his finger in a half-inch inch or so. Watching him, watch me suck on him, while I could feel the length of his erection against me, ahh, I couldn't help myself. I moaned and spread my legs some more.

Mirth danced in his eyes but his thigh pressed on me harder, teasing me deliberately. "So desperate, Jodie? Be good. A few days only."

Behave for a few *days*? I screwed up my forehead trying to convey my question.

But he only laughed. "I think you'll know what to do. Look at how well you've learnt not to speak. Think about that if anything. Think about what it does to you, not being able to talk. Say it to the camera, behave for me, and you can come."

Philosophy 101? Then I get to come? Wow.

I should have wanted to smack his face for that. But no. I would have kneeled and sucked his cock all day for how that had made me feel. Having to wait for permission to come, it just grabbed me somehow.

Slut.

You just did not do this. Not.

Why simply slut, I thought. This was more. Slave?

Documentary. I yanked myself up short with that. Remember? Pretend?

Was it though? I was finding it hard to tell. So goddamned hard. I liked this. Somehow…I liked it.

* * * *

I was good for three days. I was so good I would have made my old self vomit. I did what Klaus asked me to. I cleaned naked, I cooked naked, I kneeled at his feet, also naked. I bent over when he asked and let him touch me and I protested not at all…apart from whining when he stopped touching me. I lost count of how many times he stirred me up then left me aroused and unfulfilled. Excruciating. Yet I wanted more of what he did.

On the third morning, when he let me into the downstairs room for my morning monologue, I tried to say to the camera something of what he asked me to.

"Not being able to talk to you," I began. "What does it do to me?"

I was kneeling on the floor mattress and sitting square to the camera like some little disciple talking to her mentor or sensei. Corny, but it felt right. And I was beginning to like the feel of doing things right.

"It means I don't have to spend time wondering what to say next. If something is absolutely important to me, I think I manage to say that through body language. Yes, damn you, Klaus, I have learned to hold my tongue. I can see now that we humans tend to waste time saying a lot of stuff that is either negative or unnecessary. We waffle our way through life.

"This way..." I licked my lips and looked up at the camera from the corner of my eyes. This next bit was close to the bone for me as it made me remember him touching me intimately. "This way I can feel more. I don't get so distracted. I hear, I feel, maybe I even smell and taste things better. There. I said it." I shrugged. "That's it. That's all I figured out so far."

Funny, when I heard his footsteps coming down the stairs I realized something enormous – I'd forgotten to say anything about the documentary.

We hadn't had breakfast yet and when we reached the kitchen, I saw he'd put out all the ingredients for a big Aussie breakfast – mushrooms, bacon, eggs, tomato, the toaster and fry pan. Before I could do anything he stopped me with his hand on my arm.

"Wait. You're wearing this today." Then he squatted and gestured for me to step into a red circle of silk and chiffon. No underwear, just a skirt. The waistband came up to below my belly button. Curious, I checked with my fingers, and found the hem ended just above the lowest hint of my butt. A little red bra top made the set. He helped me on with that too and went round behind me to fasten it at the back.

"Gorgeous." I felt his hand on my curve of my ass, lifting the skirt. "Sexy and it'll just show me a hint of your little cunt when you go up the stairs. If I'm behind you. Which I will be a lot, today." There was both lust and amusement in his voice.

Then his teeth sank into the muscle between my neck and shoulder. The sudden pain transfixed me. His warm tongue licked the teeth marks. As he bit me and sucked, I shuddered. I was already moistening – a sexual reflex which now hit whenever Klaus touched me. Like I was automatically primed and prepared, ready for him. Though biting was pure distilled ecstasy.

With one arm wrapped across below my breasts, holding me still, and his hand on my hip, he used his teeth, lips and tongue to mark a trail from my nape to my shoulder. Soon I was a quivering, panting mess of a woman offering her neck for him to do anything he wanted.

"Good girl." He patted my ass one more time and I heard him step back. My neck stung nicely. In this little kitchen one proper step back meant he'd be against the wall. I gulped in a few breaths and let the haze of lust lessen before I turned.

Good girl was damned insulting, or so I used to believe. But from his mouth it now became the greatest compliment. Odd, how the mind changes. The perverse and kinky became acceptable. An insult became a compliment. What next?

In his right hand Klaus held a crop. The rectangular tip rested on the top of his bare foot. He waited for me to start breakfast. As always, that he was dressed in board shorts and T-shirt emphasized how under-dressed I was. No underwear beneath this skirt, for some weird reason made me feel even more aware of my femaleness than when I'd been naked.

If I made breakfast without being told would I get to come? The little skirt, and how carefully he'd dressed me, handled me, and that glorious biting – it made me want him *so* much I ached.

Underneath the concealing chiffon my clit was sitting up and pretty much begging. I wanted to him to make love to me. I wanted to get to come and not just be a fuck toy like the day before. Had I been good enough, though?

I eyed the crop. He hadn't hit me with anything for ages, only little pats on my behind. Like maybe he was sparing me? He cared that I was bruised? Yet I remembered how he'd adored caning me. That, I hated, but the crop, surely that couldn't hurt as much?

I...I just clicked. I wanted to see where this would lead me. Demeaning? Maybe. No worse than before, except that I was going to set it in motion.

I breathed in deeply then I went to my knees. I crawled to him and I put my hand to the crop and tugged uncertainly, afraid I looked silly. His mouth was straight and tight. His eyes blazed gray-green and fearsome. Right then you could have told me the sun was that color and I would've believed you. I swallowed, paralyzed. Then the corners of his lips curved.

He likes this.

And that, God, that thought gave rise to another – I loved pleasing him.

Klaus released the crop into my grasp. I put it in my mouth then I returned to the counter, making sure I waggled my butt as I crawled. I stood and lay on the counter as I had the morning before, then I reached back and balanced the crop across my lower back. Tantalizing, inches from my ass. I figured the picture that presented would be near on irresistible. I could feel his gaze on me there, between my legs, where I knew my lower lips were already swelling. I swallowed and waited. I was a soda pop bottle all shaken and about to explode.

And so I waited for him to decide what to do. I hazed out just a little. Waiting, forever.

Right then, I succumbed and gave myself to Klaus. The only man who'd ever made me his.

⁊ *Chapter Fourteen* ⁊

Klaus

I nearly swallowed my tongue. Maybe it shouldn't have surprised me. I knew Jodie read books about women being captured by men and subdued, sometimes even raped. She read them because something in the stories attracted her. I knew that what I'd gotten her to do would never have worked at all with many women. So why the surprise when she begged for the crop, basically flaunted her pussy at me, then presented her rear end to be cropped or fucked or whatever I wanted to do with it?

Because it was like a step into another world. A world where she had said in explicit body language, this could become us.

Damn.

I had that right didn't I?

Christ, I hoped so.

I stepped up to her, rested my hand on her butt cheek and stroked it while I retrieved my crop. I drank in everything about this position she'd assumed.

The blue sky in the window beyond and the cream counter top framed her upper body. She lay there flat with her peach-shaped ass peeking naked from under the red skirt. The line of her bare slit glistened with her moisture. The bruises on her skin were fading but still evident as dots of heavy blue black. The slope of her long legs led the eye downward to the ankle cuffs and her dainty feet. Her toes scuffled on the floor, flexing, releasing. She waited for me to act. To choose.

Under my hand her warm butt tensed and relaxed.

Some of the possibilities ran through my head. One of them was needles. I'd seen pictures on the net of them being used. I had some in the box of toys I'd collected. Sterile, unused, safe. I could see myself slowly pushing one through her skin, could feel her quiver and squeal, see her eyes dilate. My groin tightened. I gulped and cleared my throat. *Jesus. No.*

Get a grip. Some kinky shit was not meant to happen.

No. Never ever. Something else.

And how was this a documentary when I was even contemplating doing that? It wasn't, clearly. Whatever it was though, I was running with it and not stopping until I had to. I did a few experimental taps on her ass with the crop. Red slowly flared on her bite-worthy female butt. Fuck winning the lottery, I had Jodie.

I could have simply thrashed her and I would have enjoyed the whole process. I knew that about myself. But I lowered the crop to the counter. I wanted her to enjoy this too. I wanted her to join me in this adventure more than she had so far.

"Stay."

I went out and grabbed a desk chair from the study, wheeled it in, was ridiculously pleased to see she hadn't moved. After locking the wheels up, I sat.

"Come here." I beckoned.

Though hesitant at first, Jodie lay over my lap when I showed her where I wanted her. Her hands and feet on the floor kept her balanced. Frowning through a curtain of her auburn hair, she peered back at me.

After flipping up the tiny skirt to reveal all of her bare ass, I caressed both cheeks. My palm made gentle circles over the wonderful curves and down to her cleft, spreading her thighs, then I delved past the dimpled button of her anus. The instinctive wink of the muscles there gave me an idea.

Anal. That was another of Jodie's no-noes. So many of them. I planned to plow through them all.

I found her vaginal moisture. She wriggled on my knee.

"This is definitely mine today," I murmured. "Jodie's ass. All of it. I'm going to do whatever I want. First of all, I'm going to spank you."

That first little whimper was enough to squeeze my balls.

I started slow and light. Between blows, I toyed with her cleft and her clit, and soon she was writhing on my knee, and gasping at every smack. I wanted to hear her say how she felt. Wanted her to admit to how much this worked for her.

"Do you like this?"

After a swallow, came a quiet, "Yes."

I kept going. I spanked her harder and fondled her clit and her nipples. I bit the back of her neck, the muscles of her back and every place I could reach on her butt, until I had her moaning and pushing her groin onto my leg.

"Nearly there, Jodie?" She was. I didn't need an answer to that question. Her whimpers and cute sexy noises told me.

One orgasm to warm her up. Only this one came with a small price. I knew precisely how she liked her clit pressed and once I had a rhythm going I didn't let up. Her back arched up into my hand and I parked my otherwise unoccupied hand on the small of her back. Using her own juices for lubrication, I hooked the very tip of my finger into her anus and slowly, sneakily, worked it in.

I'd always loved doing this to a woman. It was so hot and tight in there. Taking Jodie anally was a dark and powerful way to make her mine.

Though she squeaked and attempted half-heartedly to get away, I leaned on her with my forearm. Then with my finger and thumb I forced the orgasm from her. A hot and incredibly long one.

Her high-pitched cries and the upward arching spasms of her back went on and on.

The best part was where my forefinger ended up. I smiled as I looked at where it was, buried to the second knuckle inside that little rosette of muscle. "I'm going to train you to take butt plugs, Jodie. In a week or so, we'll be having anal sex."

She grunted and levered herself up an inch off my lap. The word came out soft but very audible. "Nooo."

"I heard that. It's yes, and you've only made me work my finger in farther. Three strikes." I angled my eyebrow. "But you were getting those anyway. Now, the crop. And the smallest butt plug."

Sure she'd agreed to the crop, but the butt plug suggestion would make her fight. I knew that and I plain loved fighting her. With her flailing her arms, twisting, and struggling to rise, I forced her down, grabbed her wrists and locked them together. Then I clipped her ankle cuffs together. Last of all, I got up, and forced her to lean over the back of the chair so I could clip her wrist cuffs to the base of the arm rests. Her palms were set flat on the cushioned seat, her breasts were where I could feel them as needed, and her stomach rested on the thick, padded chair back. And boy, was she cross.

When I swept aside her hair to see her upside down face, her scowl would have flattened a six foot construction worker. Not me.

"Save that for someone who cares." I grinned and straightened. I interlaced my fingers, turned them inside out and stretched my finger joints. "You're all mine, darling."

She hadn't spoken again, no matter how much she hated this, she hadn't spoken. Priceless. I surveyed my little victim.

Her thighs and pink ass were right where I wanted them. Jodie was trapped and ever so croppable. I worked the chair forward so it was wedged into the corner of the cupboards, and I attached her ankle cuffs to the base of the chair. Then I took up the crop and gave it a practice swish.

"Wait there." I backed away. She couldn't go anywhere. Except… "Don't wriggle or the chair could turn over. "I'll be back in a sec."

I knew some of the rules now. The safety ones. Like don't leave anyone tied up and unsupervised for long.

∽ *Chapter Fifteen* ∾

Jodie

Okay. That wrestle had not been wise. It had knocked the stuffing out of me and made me notice all the wonderful muscles Klaus used in judo fights. The thrill I got from being beaten down had come back and possessed my body again. I detested the idea of anal in principle. It just seemed dirty. But when I'd come, inside me there'd been new sensations. Foreign, yet interesting. I closed my eyes and felt those again. My pussy squeezed in.

I still hated him making me. I tried to stamp my feet but stopped when the chair wobbled. Fuck it. Then I tried to work my hands loose anyway, and was grunting and tugging when...

"Still here?" The close warmth of his voice from a foot behind shocked me into stillness. "Move one more finger and I'll get the monster plug. Now, this is the same as my finger and it's lubricated, so you can take it."

I swore softly with every curse word I knew as he touched the center of my other hole with the tip of the plug and began to wriggle it in. Klaus laughed and said he'd have to give me amnesty for those words but that it was worth it. I barely understood. I was busy, hurting. Not in a good way.

I tensed my thighs until he whacked me and said to be silent and to push out. Yeah, knew that trick from all my stories. So, still muttering *bastard you bastard* in my head, I pushed outward down there and felt the thing slowly advance inside me. Keening deep in my throat, I labored through the burn until the plug slipped all the way in with a last painful jolt.

"Done. And by the way, it's actually a bit bigger than my finger."

Bastard!

Then he did what he had as he'd spanked me – alternated playing with my clit and my pussy in between cropping me. My butt was way up in the air, and I was staring down at the chair wondering why this position got me so turned on, and why him hitting me did it too.

The intensity of the hits built, pattering then whacking in sharp bites across all of my ass, down my thighs. The pain became one huge pulse in time with my heartbeats and a faraway blurred me whimpered and whined with every blow.

He slid his big fingers along my slit, up and down, back there where I could do nothing. I braced with my palms on the chair seat and arched my spine. One of his fingers circled in the wetness around my clit then pinched soft and steady, over and over. The pleasure throbbed higher, deeper, even spreading from where that plug was seated inside me. He reached and found my breast, smoothed the flat of his hand over the curve then tugged at my jutting nipples.

The feelings merged, rippled into waves of heat.

I bowed my head and concentrated on what he was doing to my body, between my legs. Tugging, pressing, arousing me. My toes pushed and pushed on the floor. I couldn't stop myself. Every part of me tensed and I choked out little gasps.

"Come on, girl. You can do it. Come. I've got you here as long as I want to keep you here. You're not getting away. When I'm done you are going to be fucking used up. You're already not an anal virgin. That plug is firmly stuck in your innocent asshole."

The shock of his words shuddered into me. Another series of finger pumps squeezed on my clit.

I strained at the wrist cuffs, the ankle cuffs.

"Come."

I groaned and arched more with each coaxing, cunning probe of his fingers. He covered me. His body thrust on mine, and some part of him back there, his cock perhaps, pressed and pressed on the butt plug.

"One day soon," he whispered. "It's going to be my dick in there. In your ass. And I'll make damn sure you won't be in a position to stop me."

The idea of that…

Oh fuck. I came. I cried out in rhythmic grunts as the pleasure swept me again, roaring into every muscle, filling me. He'd done this to me, possessed me. And he kept pressing on my clit though I was dying to stop climaxing.

"Oh God. Oh God. No. Stop, stop."

At last he did and I collapsed as far as I could onto the chair.

"My turn."

When he rammed up into me I was sure I felt the shock wave from the push of his cock most of the way up my body. I rocked forward in the thrusts, the chair creaked, and I groaned again. That plug was still in my anus and I couldn't stop feeling how good that was. Both holes, crammed tight. There was something supremely bad and dirty about this. My mind flashed to one of my fantasies – two men one taking me, one in my mouth, the other where Klaus was now. I held that thought as he rocked back and forth inside me.

Being penetrated from behind had always been the ultimate for me. Only now there was more, I was his fucktoy. His dirty, bad, fucktoy. So I went with the ride. I didn't hold back from showing how well he pleasured me. And I damn near came again when he did.

We lay on the floor after, spooning, our sweat mingling. I could barely open my eyes to check when Baxter came purring in the catflap and marched over.

"Here's my second pussy," Klaus said in my ear.

I chuckled, moving his arms as I laughed, those big hard-muscled arms that held me and that had made me do things I'd never have agreed to if asked. I shut my eyes and nuzzled the skin on his forearm, nibbled on him a little, while he brushed aside my sweaty hair and kissed me below the collar.

A thought wormed its way into my mind. Right then, I was where I wanted to be, but it had to end. It had to end someday. This couldn't last.

Above us the camera light blinked from where he'd installed yet another camera. Not that we could use most...hardly any...of the footage. Unless we made a porno flick. I'd be doing a ton of editing.

If I was normal, my more sensible self added, I'd have fled by now. I'd have found a time when he didn't have me tied up and I'd have gone. What if the next thing he wanted me to do was dangerous or just too much? There was no allowance for saying no in any of what Klaus did. I might lose a finger, a limb, or my mind.

I liked living on the edge of danger, though. It was why the stage attracted me. How boring was life if you only went with the safe? I pondered all this as I lay there with Klaus leaning across me and patting Baxter. Now that cat was worse than me. He'd purr for anyone who fed him.

Me, I shut my eyes and smiled...right now, it was only Klaus who made me purr.

∽ Chapter Sixteen ∾

Klaus

I sat on one of the weather-proof steel benches near the jetty and watched the catamaran cruise into the bay. As it backed to get everything squared away and the off-ramps lined up, the muted rumble of the big engines sounded like a predator warning away other beasts. Once the ropes were dropped over the bollards, the tourists surged out. Soon I was surrounded by a crowd. Mostly these were young families out for a day on the island. Kids screamed and ran about in their bright shorts, tops or dresses. Many people had snorkels and flippers, or ice boxes chock full of holiday gear. The seagulls were having fun pouncing on the potato fries thrown aside by giggling children.

And I was the outsider. I was a sadist. In my basement, I had a mostly naked woman who I beat regularly.

I remembered this disjointed feeling from the last time, from every time, I ventured out. My two shopping bags lay next to my feet. Milk, eggs, orange juice and various other items, including another selection of clothes that could be tossed when I tired of them, or mutilated to my heart's content. And there was some string to tie up the nipples of the woman I'd left in the room.

Was I fucking insane?

I had a good job, great income, an honest reputation – not bad for a taxation accountant. Two and a half more weeks and my locum –

the accountant who was filling in for me – was off to Europe. I had to go back to work then.

I knew why I didn't let Jodie talk, still. It wasn't for the wonderful reason she'd discovered. It was partly because I was afraid of what she might tell me if face to face and allowed to say whatever she wished. Partly too, because I got off on the power dynamic.

This way that I just *took* from her whatever I wanted was wrong, morally, ethically, even logically. But I didn't want to stop when the time was over.

Maybe she'd agree to this continuing?

I'd figured out one of the local kinksters on Fetlife was a close friend from the kayaking club I used to be in. His pic, if you knew him well, was a dead giveaway. Only on Fetlife his name was Moghul. He was a Dom, and a font of information. Not all of it was useable. If I told him what we were truly doing, I think he would have been horrified. Jodie and I had something different happening. Something better.

I stared out across the beach. Seagulls were squawking indignantly as a small boy chased them. He ran in circles giggling insanely. His mother sat cross-legged on a towel nearby, smiling at his antics. She had a pile of seashells by her foot and the usual colorful plastic toys and shovel.

We'd strolled along this beach once, Jodie and I. The island only had so many beaches. She'd collected shells too, but when it had been time to get on the ferry, instead of dropping the shells, or taking them with us, she'd gifted the lot to a little girl in a blue dress and floppy hat. As she'd carefully tipped them into the girl's chubby hand, then picked up a couple that had fallen onto the sand, I'd grinned. It had made me wonder about Jodie, about whether she would ever be a mother, and if I could ever be a father.

I guess I'd been hoping it would be us, together, but it was so long ago I couldn't remember that part. Maybe I'd blocked it out.

I stood, picked up the bags, and headed for the jeep. Like every time I was out, I was growing nervous about leaving her alone. I might have loved hurting her, but I didn't want her trapped in the house while it burned. Or…

I halted, struck by a ridiculous thought. What if an intruder broke in and assaulted her?

I'd kill him.

Crazy. To care and yet to want to hurt.

I still hadn't figured out where I fitted in this whole scenario. Was I turning into the bad guy? Beneath all her protests, Jodie liked what I did. I was certain of that.

But I did have to ask her about this continuing, didn't I?

Yeah, I did. Determination went *kerthunk* as it landed in the front of my mind. As long as her answer was yes.

Yep, I was insane. Knew it.

But I'd ask her. Because it was the right thing to do.

* * * *

Before I went down to the basement room, I sat in the living room to hear Jodie's latest monologue. If she ever made a film, if I let her, these were what she'd have to use as the backbone. Not the footage of us having crazy sex. Or of me beating her until she screamed.

Her last words made me rewind the film, turn up the volume, and lean in.

She was kneeling as always, perfect position, but looking at the floor, then she looked up directly at the camera. Her light blue eyes were wide, unblinking.

"I've lost track of time, Klaus. I need to know how much longer before our time is up. I want to talk about us, about weaning ourselves away from…" She gestured vaguely. "From all this. You know we have to? Yes?"

Hell. I sat back, paused the film, and stared at her in freeze frame.

What could I do?

I'd been all set to talk but this showed me she was already on the wrong side of the equation. And I knew from the past all about talking with Jodie. I'd talked to her about her drinking, and about toning down her stage persona so she wasn't feeling compelled to spew forth everything that went wrong in her life. I'd talked about how she related to me and about how looking after one another went both ways. She hadn't changed. Talking didn't work so well.

Communication was the very bedrock of BDSM according to Moghul, but there were other ways of communicating. If I talked, she would likely reject my ideas. The funny thing about saying no was that it set up a barrier in the mind so that a yes became much harder to say.

We'd been doing this a while. Weeks.

Stockholm Syndrome. Where was that when you needed it?

And those other ways of communicating?

Showing, *doing*, was far superior to talking. You could always talk later, when she knew what it was like to experience it for real. After all, a wish to try out what she'd read in books had led Jodie to this.

Two and a half weeks left. I found myself with the remote in hand, turning it like a pig on a spit. I wasn't some serial killer murderer, kidnapper sort, but there was nothing about weaning in our agreement. Technically, I had that time to do what I wanted to.

I had that time to convince her to keep going. In whatever way I could imagine. I'd barely scratched the surface of what was possible.

Those other ideas materialized. I could do them. She wanted to see what it was like to be a slave. I could show her.

Really? I stared at the remote, then stared at the TV some more. I really wanted to do this?

My certainty faltered. I wanted to. But I suspected it was wrong. But I was going to.

Maybe if I was another man, I'd have been thinking about how to talk her into a relationship after the documentary ended. I would have been talking with her, full stop. But the opposite course of action drew me like gravity on a man falling from the sky. I was going down, down, down.

I'd never thought of myself as the obsessive sort, yet I knew all the way down to my toenails that I could not back away from this without trying to the utmost. I wanted this so deeply it hurt. I wanted to own her. Not in some mock BDSM scene way. I really wanted her as mine. To do with as I pleased. Crack had *nothing* on this.

Moghul was hosting a party in about two weeks, on the Sunday – the last day of this so-called documentary. The temptation was too much. Train her. Take her to the play party and show her how suitable she was to be my pet. Jodie already had the collar; all she needed was the right moves, and the right attitude.

ᚽ Chapter Seventeen ᚽ

Jodie

I heard his words as he strode into the room, but they were so outrageous, so unexpected, after what I'd just requested on camera, that I had to replay them in my head.

Right now, you're my captive and time does not exist.

I focused on him again and stiffened – the leather straps, the spider gag, and the cane in his hand. He looked so formidable.

My thoughts were…seriously, my first thoughts were laced with fear.

What had I done? I shifted on my knees.

Clearly, to him, I'd done wrong.

He squatted beside me. His trousers were tight across his thighs, his hands rested there with the cane and that nasty spider gag. I hated it and couldn't help eyeing it, as if it were some venomous creature.

"This is how it will be. Obeisance when I enter a room." He pulled my head forward until I overbalanced and slapped my hands to the floor. "Down. Forehead on the floor. Hands way out in front with your arms outstretched. Don't speak."

I knew what an obeisance was. A slave did it for their Master.

His commanding growl had me obeying and lying in a sort of flat bow with my knees tucked under me. Worrying about the documentary could wait. I'd reacted as always. I'd warmed down below. Traitorous clit. It must be an ingrained response from wanking to all those fantasy books. Precisely this scenario would have had me flipping the ebook pages one-handed.

Not speaking had become easy. So it startled me when he set the spider gag in my mouth and buckled it on. Using the same hand-in-hair grip he dragged my head up. Instinctively, whining at the pain, I put my hands up.

"Hands at your back!" he snapped.

Chastised, I put them there, lacing my fingers together to give me pause in case I forgot.

"From now on, for whatever length of time I choose, you are my pet. No words. No getting on furniture. No getting up on your feet. Not unless I say you can."

He didn't ask for an answer but I grunted once, blinking watery-eyed, because of the sting from the pull on my hair.

"First lesson. You are available when I say. Don't move anything." One-handed he unzipped, took out his erect cock and put it to my mouth, then slowly thrust inside past the metal of the gag. He tasted of the sea and I felt grains of sand rub on my lips. As he fucked my mouth, I wondered, strangely, if he'd been swimming while I'd been stuck in this room. Then, after a few thrusts, he pushed my forehead to the floor again and went behind me. Within seconds his cock was sliding into me there.

Oh God. Used. Taken. Something about the casual assumption of my body being his, my mouth or any other part of me, resonated inside my soul.

Those first few seconds of entry, especially when I could do little to stop him, it scattered me, all I could feel was *him* in there, his flesh opening up mine as he pushed inward.

"You can brace your hands on the floor," he ground out, having paused at the bottom of the stroke, imbedded in me all the way.

I groaned and wriggled a little, but did as he said, flopping my arms out and curling my fingers against the floor as if I could grab onto it. This time he plowed me for longer than he had my mouth, but before he came, he pulled out and zipped up. I was head to the floor with my butt in the air and screaming inside for him to continue. You could have handed me to a football team and I would have welcomed them. I was that turned on. He rode rough shod over me. He callously, with no regard for my opinion, had decided what should be done with my body. I was hot as hell. Incandescent maybe.

Guess I liked being objectified.

"Up. Off the floor." He smacked me damn hard, once, on my rear.

I let out a soft moan before shuffling to my knees and looking at him wistfully. Whatever plans he had, so far I liked them. I remembered that I trusted him. So, therefore, he knew the time left for our documentary, but wasn't telling me. Okay, I could roll with that.

Though his next actions perplexed me. Leaving me where I was in the middle of the room, he went and turned off the camera. Then he came to me and taped my hands up so my fingers were together like mittens.

"Every day I'll do that until special mittens arrive. You no longer have hands to use. Pets don't need them." He bent and kissed me hard enough to hurt my lips, then he went down on his knees and bit and sucked my ass hard enough to make me try to get away. I couldn't, of course. Laughing, he held me down and finished what he meant to. Now I had a new circular bruise. I glared. Drool from the gag dribbled to the floor.

"Marked. Good." He poked the bruise once and casually fingered me between my legs. "I might get you tattooed somehow in the future. Something that makes you mine."

Shit, shit, shit. Not in my book. No way.

"Don't glare at your Master."

Master?

Then he tipped me and rolled me onto my belly.

"Hands at your back. Fast!" The grating harshness of his words told me how close he was to taking me again.

I would've begged if I could have. Lust choked me, made me so aware of my vulnerability, of the moisture slicking my folds, and of how easy it would be for him to thrust his cock or fingers into me without me being able to do anything much to stop him.

"Good." Like the inspector of some animal, he put his splayed hands either side on the cheeks of my ass then used his thumbs to stretch my lower lips, opening me to his gaze.

I moaned softly. *Fuck me, please.* My wrists were against each other, my eyes were closed, and I waited, heating up more and more with each passing moment. I knew where he was looking.

I heard the rip of tape being peeled from a roll and then a second later he taped my wrists together. While I was testing the inescapability of those bonds, the cane smacked down on my butt. With no warm-up the pain bit hard. Squealing and screaming only made him hit me again. Eventually I stayed silent and trembled, and took the last few blows only shuddering and gasping wetly into the floor.

Something had changed. I could sense an edgier purpose in what he did.

Fear crept into my bones and whispered to me, dark things.

"Count the stairs," he said, as he hauled me up the stairs with a hand under my arm and the leash at my collar. "I will test you."

Count?

I counted. Apparently I got it wrong, because after he went back and counted them too, he came up the stairs and caned me, again. The lines on my butt were lines of fire. Then he fucked my mouth again until I gagged, untaped my hands, then got me to do the dishes while my head was whirling. I was to count the dishes too, as I went, even when he put a vibe to my clit and got me off, gasping, crouched over the sink.

After that he lubed a small butt plug and inserted it. He came inside me while I sluiced out a cup. I wasn't to move, or break anything. That cup got washed well. Round and round the sponge went for at least five minutes until I gave in and just held on tight. Dishwater sloshed out of the sink. I was punished, for grabbing the tap to keep myself still. Gasping sounds odd when you have a spider gag in.

The mess that dripped down my leg as I went back to washing and drying, I had to clean up after, and I had to count the tiles on the floor under the mop. Ever so dirty. Ever so wrong. Strange. And yet the times when I had the gag off, it hadn't occurred to me to say no or stop.

I got good at counting over the next few days. From the tick of the second-hand on the clock at my back, to the timber floor boards I washed, to the teeth on the zipper of his pants. I counted them all, got some wrong. I mean really, *teeth* on a zipper?

Sometimes he used the cane, sometimes it was clothes pins on my nipples or labia, or my tongue. I hurt everywhere. I had orgasms by the dozen some days. The vibe used up all our batteries and he went away to get more. Then the package arrived with my new leather mittens he could buckle on instead of tape and take off if he needed to. In the same package was a huge massager that he commenced using to bring me to orgasm faster than anyone should orgasm. I found out my clit could go numb.

My clit and mouth and pussy were well used. Numbers ran through my head all day. The exercise bike I had tucked away in a storage cupboard was dragged out and I was allotted times to exercise. Klaus alternated so that every second day I was deprived of sight, of sound, and of normality.

Ear plugs, black goggles, mittens, I began to feel ever more disconnected from reality. I could hear, but sound was muted. I couldn't see at all. I could only feel the insides of the leather mittens and rub my fingers against one another.

On those days the only time I was alone was in the toilet. Sometimes I wondered if I was sleeping at night or in the day. After one occasion when he caught me peeking from beneath the goggles and punished me with the cane, I gave in. Besides, the world was simpler behind them. I only had to breathe, and count, be fed delicacies by Klaus, and be fucked and have orgasms.

No money worries, no traffic, no stupid lame conversations with people you never wanted to meet again. No worry, at all. Even my existence seemed up to him. If some disaster happened, I'd have to rely on him to get us out alive.

But the thing that seeped into my consciousness above all was what I valued most on the days when I *could* see, and that was being able to serve him. We exchanged smiles, he bestowed on me loving caresses and kisses, and I knew I was the focus of his world as much as he was of mine. If I had to put my finger on it, I guess I'd grown to like giving of myself to him.

When I knelt and offered him a meal I'd prepared, and saw pleasure in his eyes, that was fulfillment. When he let me up on the lounge to be petted while he watched TV, I was grateful. Yet when I had to curl up on a pillow at his feet, I was just as happy. I'd changed so much. I knew the how and the why behind this change, and I didn't care. I could see so much more in selflessness than I could ever have imagined as the woman I once was. I came to wonder if this was a form of love.

On some days, everything faded and I merely *was*. I existed. When I came to think about it, I knew that he'd aimed for this – I was his, nothing more.

I pined for things of course. Sometimes I wanted to choose. I wanted the variety of life beyond this. But it was still there. When I was ready, when Klaus was ready, we would return to it. I knew this. What I had now was unique. The pain he liked, it had less hold on me too. I'd learnt to bear it, and even, sometimes, to ride it into the realm of pleasure.

But one day I had an idea. A bad one. I thought of a way to escape. With Klaus away at the shop, I realized I'd not heard the usual click of the door. He'd left me in the basement room with the goggles on and ear plugs in. Knocking the goggles awry with my mittened hands was easy. I blinked and looked about, dizzy for a second as my balance mechanism reasserted itself. It always happened to me after long periods blind.

The ear plugs could wait until I got the mittens off. And wow, the door was ajar by an inch and not locked. On the floor I spied a splinter of timber caught between the door and the door frame, stopping the door closing. Glee possessed me at the danger of what I was doing. He could only beat me if he caught me. I nudged through the door with my shoulder and padded up the stairs, half-naked, in a bikini top and one of the skirts he liked. No panties.

Curious, I checked – polka dot blue and white this time. Huh. I had a notion he got these second-hand. It explained why he discarded them so easily.

The back kitchen door was deadlocked. Perhaps the front door? Or the garage door? That one would do. I couldn't use a key but I could press the garage door button, surely?

Almost giggling with delirium, I went down the other short flight of steps into the garage. The button was on the center column. I approached it and stopped, thinking. Unused brain cells chugged back to life.

Crap. How clueless had I become? I couldn't go out as I was. I needed underwear. I needed, I held my mittened hands before my eyes, to get *these* off. My heart pitter-pattered double time. Where was I going? What would I do out there? Was this the end of our experiment? The anxiety that arose was so stupendously ridiculous that more amusement bubbled up. I was worried about being normal? *But, do I really want to stop?*

Because I liked where I was.

I hadn't made a choice, a decision, in days, weeks. I hadn't needed to think ahead. I swallowed, shifted from one bare foot to the other.

The ear plugs didn't block out everything, they just made things quieter.

The grinding hum of the door motor made me jump. The door bottom lifted, showing a widening sliver of bright sunlight. Gravel clacked as the jeep drew up. I could see tires, then the face of the driver, of Klaus. Frozen in place, I stayed where I was as he drove in, opened the door and stepped out.

Big. He was big, muscular, and cross. I swallowed.

The garage floor was concrete with chips of rock and grit. I didn't hesitate a second longer. I dropped and prostrated myself in obeisance, and I waited, shaking.

Did I shake from fear or some sort of adrenalin high? Even I wasn't sure.

He knelt on one knee beside me and gently, with his hand under my chin, encouraged me to raise my head. "Been bad, pet?"

His gray-green eyes looked somehow puzzled, yet the longer I met his gaze the more it changed to that familiar sadistic and evil one. The one that he wore when he walked about marking me with the crop or the cane.

On cue, the tingles of arousal trickled straight to my clit.

"Yes-s." I was a mouse. A mouse with goosebumps prickling cold down her arms, and with heat gathering in her groin. *Whip me, beat me, I've been bad.* "I'm sorry."

"You will be."

The promise in those words made me inhale sharply and bite my lip.

⚘ *Chapter Eighteen* ⚘

Klaus

The needles – since I'd told her she'd be sorry, I'd been imagining using them as punishment.

This is wrong, had been going round and round in my head for ages. Should I, would I?

I wanted to do it so much. This would all end sometime soon. It was a good punishment. Maybe too good. Was it wrong? I still hadn't figured that out. I hadn't decided if I would use them.

I hadn't tied her in bondage this restrictive for ages. From the couch, I watched her little squirms, as she tested the ropes to get loose. The unhappy pout and tiny scowl she sent my way had me striving not to grin. I loved that. Knowing it wasn't quite what she expected added to the satisfaction I got from all this.

Where I had her sitting in the center of the dining table on the mattress, she doubled as a decorative centerpiece.

The shibari I'd done was beautiful, pushing out her breasts like ripe fruit. Perched in the middle were those pink-brown targets – lures for my tongue and mouth. Simply tying her, binding her, into position had stirred my girl and five minutes ago her nipples had been standing up pert and tight. Now they were flat but that only made her areola look shinier and succulent. They seemed to beg me to go over there and suck them. My dick twitched at the thought. I could taste them already, I knew them that well.

I had such a good idea for tonight. I'd been thinking about this for days, wondering if I should go there. Like Moghul recommended, I'd tested them on my own skin to make sure I could do this. Ouch for sure. But I had my experience helping out Jon now and then at his vet clinic on the island. His nurses tended to be away on the mainland on weekends, and as a regular fellow kayaker, I'd gotten to know him well on my early morning stints.

A pang of regret hit me. I missed being able to do those. An hour out paddling on the ocean with Jodie left here alone? No. I couldn't do that.

At any rate, I'd become nonchalant about sticking needles into animals, so why not people, or women in particular? It wasn't that difficult to use needles. And now, I had the best excuse ever. Punishment. I put my arm along the back of the couch and contemplated her some more as I decided.

She whimpered enticingly and wriggled.

The midway point of the rope looped at the back of her neck then went down and wrapped about her chest, circumnavigating each breast before the rope continued on down and dived between her legs. Her knees were folded up and strapped; her wrist cuffs were clicked to the outsides of the thigh cuffs. She was bent over like a little package. Every entry I wanted access to was available in an instant. But it was her breasts I wanted first.

I waited some more, pretending to concentrate on the TV, when really, I was going over what she'd done today. It had scared me. Not because of what it might have revealed to others, but because of what it had shown me about myself. During the minute or two while I'd driven in and exited the jeep, I'd been as insecure as a man clinging to a cliff edge by his fingernails. And I hadn't been quite sure why.

If she'd gotten away, it would be before I could explain about anything, about my feelings. I figured that was it. Trouble was, I still didn't know what to say. I want to hurt you, but I care for you? How dumb did that sound? I shook my head. Leave it.

On the coffee table the crop waited for me along with other implements such as the diamante nipple clamps, the clothes pins and the belt. I hoped to use them all on her. Soon. This needed to be a lesson. A slave caught attempting to escape, would expect to be punished. Which was why I also had the packet of needles. Twenty-five gauge. Tiny, but not as fine as acupuncture needles. I picked up the plastic zip lock bag, tossed it high, caught it. She paled.

"You know what these are?" When she didn't answer, I rose, gathered up the other items and crossed to the table where I deposited everything at one end, a few feet from Jodie. "Do you know?" I opened the bag and removed ten of the needles.

"Of course," she croaked, rocking a little on her legs. "I don't want –"

"Enough."

Though she licked her lips she stayed silent. A thrill ran through me, all the way to my dick. One word and she was quiet, even in the face of this, something she obviously dreaded. Right now, I was king to her. And not because she feared me more than the needles. I knew she didn't. It was from pure habit.

I went to her and gently laid her on her back on the mattress. Folded as her thighs were, sitting up might be hurting her.

I checked her feet for circulation trouble – for color and capillary refill. As a precaution, I undid the straps for a minute and massaged her legs, then refastened the bondage. She waited patiently, like a little doll.

Once I had her again how I wanted her, I studied her. Naked. A woman I could do with as I wished. In-fucking-credible.

I wrapped my hand about her ankle, held on tightly so she knew it was I who had command of her. A shiver shook her body. My nostrils dilated, my gaze focused minutely on her. I was the predator here. *I.* How many men in this day and age got to be as primeval as this? I could never explain this, how much it drew me. I doubted even Moghul understood.

"Do you deserve punishment, Jodie? For trying to escape?"

She squeezed shut her eyes then opened them again. I could see her ice blue orbs as she regarded me. Her lips parted. Her face was reddened and she breathed in tight bursts that lifted her breasts toward me. I placed my palm on the nearest one and waited. Her nipple crinkled. Then its partner followed. In the depths of her eyes, there seemed fear, astonishment, even lust.

"Jodie?"

"Oh God." She shook her head, swallowed. Her voice was still raspy, as if she'd been out screaming at some rock concert. While I waited for her to gather herself, I shifted some strands of hair that had strayed into her mouth and across her nose.

"I...Yes. I do. I'm sorry." Her forehead wrinkled. She shifted as if testing the secureness of the straps. "I don't know why. This is...madness. But I want you to punish me." Her words dropped into a whisper. "I don't know why but I do." Tears leaked from the corners of both eyes and ran down her face into her hair.

Hell. Transfixed, I stared back. I had not expected that reply. *She wants this? I'm lost now. How can I let her go?*

I bent and I kissed her softly, and still I could barely conceive of what the whirl of thoughts in my head meant. Why did this mean so much to me? *She wants this?* Then she kissed me back, avidly. I spent time worshipping at her lips before I pulled away. By then my erection was hard as rock and Jodie was flushed even more, and panting.

I found the alcohol wipes and cleaned off her areola. She peered downward, her tongue curled up against her upper lip. When I plucked the first needle from its cap, she whined a little, barely audible but it was there. I paused, head down, thinking. To reassure her, or not?

The urge struck me to ask her if she trusted me. Why then? No idea. Trust though. There'd been a time I'd taught her how to do an eskimo roll to right a kayak if she got flipped underwater. I'd asked her if she trusted me just before I turned the kayak over. She'd said, yes. But I didn't dare ask her now because I didn't want to hear her say no.

I figured I knew the mind fuck would send her flying if I did it right. That she'd enjoy it in that odd way she seemed to like it when I plowed through her protests. Yeah, really, deep down, she liked most of what I did. I was sure of that. Even, perversely, when she didn't like it, she liked it.

I grinned. Damn. That thinking was so fucked. I was like Jodie, things in my head were not adding up.

I showed her the point of the needle, letting it shine in the overhead fluorescent light. "This, one just this size, I tried on my own skin. It hurts, but it's bearable. Okay?"

"Nooo. Not okay." Her eyebrows jerked as if a storm of emotions tore at her.

I leaned in and poised it an inch from her skin. "I know how to give injections safely. You understand that?" She nodded but her lip trembled. "I didn't try it on my nipple, though." I smiled evilly. "I'm not that keen. Now. Stay very, very still. This will only go in shallow and skim along under the skin for less than an inch, then come out."

When I advanced the needle closer to her, she flinched, of course. Flinched too much for this to be safe. "You can speak for now. Until I say to stop."

"Uh. Then, no. No, no. no. I don't want this."

"Are you going to stay still?"

"No," she squeaked out, quietly. "I can't."

So I brought out more rope and a long strap, and I tied her to the table. Tied her breasts down too. She couldn't shift far. Took ten minutes, but I did it. This time, when I approached her nipple, she could only watch, and whimper.

I wasn't aiming to damage the precious milk ducts that a woman needed to feed a child, so I aimed a tiny distance from the nipple itself.

The needle tip pierced her areola, and slid beneath to the accompaniment of her high-pitched keen.

"Fuck. No, Klaus. Shit, shit. That hurts!"

"That's the whole idea."

I started on the next needle, slipped it in, along, and exited. By now she was only muttering fuck in a long stream under her breath.

"No more words, Jodie. You can take it."

She gulped and nodded. Sweat beaded on her forehead.

"Good."

I worked fast after that, and slid in four around each nipple. Eight in total. The tightness in her eyes said pain, but her high-pitched noises had become no louder. I'd thought of attaching these via string to eyebolts above, but no, too dangerous. Instead I looped string from her nipples to the D-ring on her collar and drew them in tight.

"Move too much and you'll pull the needle upward. Got that?"

She whined a yes at me.

"Good." I cradled her jaw, stroked along the line of the bone with my thumb. "Because I aim to make you want to wriggle and squeak. Though I can't lick these anymore since you're a damn porcupine." I flicked her nipple with my fingernail. "I can do other things to you."

I drifted my hand downward from her neck, caressed both breasts, smoothing the underside, weighing them, playing some more. Because they were mine. Her breathing slowed, deepened. I could see her surprise at the awakening of arousal. I moved my hand lower, taking my time. Her belly button served as a waypoint as I circled and circled it. Then down across her belly, and into the territory of her mons. She was bare – I kept her that way and shaved her most days. I smiled. From the apex of her slit, I could already spy her clit poking its way out.

Her breasts looked pretty circled by the needles. There was no blood apart from the tiniest blebs. All was good. Damn though. Now I couldn't use the nipple clamps.

"I'll be back." I kissed the side of her breast.

Quickly I went around the table, undoing all the extra ropes and strap, careful not to catch anything on the points of the needles. The massager got plugged in next and I advanced on Jodie.

"You are not to come," I said sternly. "If you do, I may decide to use more needles. Clear?"

"Yes, Sir."

Shit. I hadn't asked her to call me anything like that. Not for days. She wasn't talking so what was the point. Sir. It sounded good. I think a fire was burning behind my eyes by then. Certainly Jodie, after one short period of meeting me eye-to-eye, flinched and kept her focus elsewhere.

"Sir, sounds good. Use that in future."

Her reply was weak. "Yes, Sir."

Oh fuck. I'm done. I'm caught. Who was the captor here? Me or her?

I was an accountant. A fucking good accountant. But, I regarded Jodie, tied up, nipples stuck with my needles, flushed, breathing hard, and with her cuffed thighs spread far apart, showing me how much her slit glistened with moisture. Little muscle movements in her thighs betrayed her. She wanted this. Needles, all that, whatever. She was aroused and quivering.

So much for punishment. I laughed inside. Orgasm denial would have to be enough. I turned on the massager and prepped her well. I cruised the vibrating head over her – body, breasts, inner thighs, and around her clit, until she was begging me with urgent eyes and moans. I played it on her clit in bursts. I finger fucked her slowly in between times when I turned it off.

Her G spot was swollen up inside there. I paid it some attention, then left it alone. Jodie trembled, groaned and strained so hard I swear I heard the thigh cuffs creak.

With her sweaty and whimpering, I stepped back, dragged off my T-shirt, undid my pants, and tossed them aside, then slipped off my underwear last of all. My cock was standing up like a flagpole by then. I was so stiff. I'd been aching to fuck her for the last hour. If anyone should have been groaning it was me.

"Nothing hurting in your legs?" I wasn't concerned about her arms, they weren't tight or folded. "Pins and needles?" Her color everywhere was normal.

"Noo. I just want to come. Sir."

Damn it. For calling me that again, I nearly let her. I cleared my throat, gripped my cock. "No. Do not come. Not. Okay?"

"Yess." Her word quavered. "I'll try."

"No. You will not!"

"Yes," she replied weakly.

"Good girl." I hauled her to the edge of the table.

I aimed at her entrance, and sank in balls deep in one long glide that made me close my eyes in appreciation. Her cunt fitted me tightly. Wet, juicy, and hot as a volcano.

"Damn," I gasped out.

I opened my eyes and leaned over her, still deep within. The string to her nipples was taut. Her back bowed off the table, her lower spine arched upward too but her thighs had fallen open in utter surrender. I pumped a few times, watching her closely, watching her quiver and sigh and moan. Her small grunts of pleasure were adorable.

I thumped in harder, thrilling at the spasms I felt on my cock and the wet sounds from her pussy as I shunted in and out. That I could put needles in her and still get her like this…damn that spoke to my bones. Loved it.

I fucked her long and hard until I came so explosively I wondered if my eyeballs were going to be sucked away. I collapsed partly over her. My shaking forearms rested either side of her on the table and I could barely stay up. Exhausted. Her little weak noise made me raise my head.

"What?"

"Can I come now? Please? Sir?"

"No." I grinned at her pitiful expression. "No. You may not." Damn, maybe I was evil.

I figured I was fit enough to do the Olympics after that. And I decided I would torture her some more, for the next three days. No orgasms but loads of teasing. It would make the day after all of that ever so much more interesting. She'd be twitching in her sleep if I did it right. I grinned to myself.

Now to take out those needles. I wondered if it would hurt her pulling them out. And then I wondered if she'd come when I did. If she did, I'd excuse her just that once. Some things were worth seeing.

She didn't orgasm. By the time I pulled on the last needle, she might have been in subspace. She barely gasped when I inched out the shiny steel. Her skin tented outward as if clinging to the point. I laid aside the needle, gently kissed her lips. Rope slid on rope. Knots unknotted. Clips were unclicked. The mechanics and humble use of my muscles to free her sank me. Thoughts twisted, slowed. Serenity flowed in.

Blinking, I undid the last piece of rope. I set my hands on her and rolled her onto her back. Her flesh rocked as I massaged her limbs. Her eyes stayed closed. Satiated, sweaty, my captive.

What better reward than this: her, as mine? I smiled. Soft as the drift of a breeze, I drew the knuckles of my hand down her cheekbone, and I rolled open her lip.

Then her eyes opened. I stared into that wonderland. This time I didn't see blue. I saw sea. I saw sky. I saw the outside world, the fracture between now and what might be.

This was ending.

Pain seized my chest.

Breathe.

And I fell again, into the real. For the first time in many weeks, I let the old me return. We had to stop. No. *I* had to. Because I wasn't sure Jodie knew how to anymore.

I played with her lip and she licked my thumb, slowly, my little trusting animal. I found courage. She wasn't mine, or not for much longer.

Weaning meant slow withdrawal, right? At the end of the next three days, I'd talk.

The goggles and the mittens could go first. The next morning, the skimpy clothes would go. Sure. I'd do it then.

That night, I let her sleep beside me, the last night as my pet.

But temptation clung to me. My mindset as her Master, ditto.

The morning tested me.

When she knelt before me, naked, after stripping herself of the skirt and bra – no man could resist that. I bent and kissed her sweetly as I cupped her pussy and fondled between her legs. God, those soft moans. I'd wean all right. I'd tease her like I'd thought to. She wouldn't come, but neither would I. We'd both learn control.

"Obeisance," I croaked, pushing her down. I went behind and nestled my cock there in that moist valley, listened to the signs that told of her arousal, of her body readying itself for me. I fastened her to the floor with a palm on the small of her back and I squeezed my cock in slow.

If I didn't come, we were getting somewhere. I would not hurt her. I could hold that part of me back. I hissed and sucked my dick back out, just as slow as it went in. My hips shook like an earthquake was imminent.

No sadism. For three days.

My head would burst if I kept this up and didn't come. I withdrew, and stood. I tucked myself away, zipped myself up. There, was that not control?

"I can do this," I whispered. At the end of three days, we'd sit and we'd talk. I'd get her used to just being mine. With that as a basis, and her predilection for BDSM activities, we'd have a starting point. Like Moghul said – talk, find your common ground. The man knew more than I did about this, surely?

It was hard though. And Jodie didn't make it any easier. On the second day I went out for milk and bread. Opening the door I found her waiting for me like I'd told her to days before, and forgotten to rescind. She lay belly down, draped over the small hall table, naked, with her legs apart just enough for me to have a clear view of her vulva.

Heart thumping, I placed the plastic bag with the groceries on the floor, and I stepped up to her. The curves of her pale ass led the eye to her nude sex. The split there was cradled by the subtle ridges of her labia. A hint of dampness glistened. The opening gaped.

What man could resist? Slowly, I unzipped my pants. She had the side of her face on the table and at the sound of the zip, her eyelashes fluttered, her lips parted. Her ass swayed the tiniest amount. She'd put on bright red lipstick. New. Her own idea. Once upon a time, I'd told her how alluring that was.

Afterward, I wondered. Had I deliberately, subconsciously, known she would wait for me like that if I forgot to say don't? As penance, I made sure to tell Moghul that I...we wouldn't be coming to the play party he had arranged. We weren't ready for it. I hadn't even told her about it.

The third day, I was more restrained. One more day and this was over. One more day. *Jesus.* I gave her back her denim shorts and top, but I had to tell her to put on bra and underwear. The look she gave me was piercing. We both knew.

How did you end a capture fantasy documentary that had gone off the rails like this had? I sure as hell didn't know. My attraction for her hadn't lessened as I'd hoped. It had multiplied a thousand times and mutated. I had changed. Jodie had. She still wasn't talking to me, because I hadn't told her to. Interesting how she held to that.

Of course we couldn't keep on as we had. I'd known that, though I'd managed to keep myself from remembering ninety-nine percent of the time. And yet, I found myself looking at her, wondering...if.

But then, what would I be? She would be a prisoner of mine and I would be imprisoned by my own mind. I had to change this. It wasn't legal or right.

That night I would tell her she could speak. I'd thought and thought about how to do this. I hadn't touched the cameras, or the footage on the hard drive, or the kinky and fetish gear scattered about the house. But I had thought for ages, through the bleak cool hours of the night, head in hands, staring at her sleeping on my bed.

If I did this right, I could keep her. It was a mental thing. Obviously. Let things slip the wrong way and she'd feel she could get the upper hand. I needed to loosen the reins, but not by too much. What we'd had was untenable anyway. I couldn't have her blinded and gagged forever, could I? We could be partners, not equal, but partners.

I wanted a woman I could discuss things with. To live life with. It was natural to want that, and I did.

The other, though, wasn't a want, it was an obsessive *need* – my need to hurt, to dominate. Pandora's Box had been opened.

Needs could be controlled. It took determination, and patience, and made me feel like I was locked in a box with wet cement pouring in, but I could do this, even if the pressure burst my head.

Find a solution. There must be one.

Okay, I'd let my darkest desires out for a while. Now they could damn well go back into hiding until I called them again.

So I set up her little circular timber table in the garden, dusted it, and arranged the two wrought iron chairs, the candles, and the lacy white tablecloth that matched her flowing dress. I took five minutes to just breathe and still my trembling hands.

Then I brought her out.

At my gesture, she hesitantly sat, sweeping her dress from beneath her out of the way of the chair.

This Indonesian-style dress I'd found in the usual place except this one was demure and ended in a hem that sloped sideways from knee to calf. Gold stitching decorated the front. A row of cloth-covered white buttons closed it all the way to her waist. Her breasts threatened to burst from the scooped neckline if she inhaled too hard.

She was beautiful.

And I yearned to tear the dress from her. I bunched my fists.

Simmer down. Count. Count to fifty. Math came to my rescue. By fifty I still had a steel-hard erection but I was calmer.

Never had I had this problem before. I was set in my ways, I guess. A month of fucking her when I wanted, making her my slave, and I regarded her as property, to do with as I wanted.

"Stay there, please," I growled. Then I walked away.

We were barefoot, but I'd dressed in a button-down shirt and black pants. The Thai restaurant had done a great selection of food, and I dished it up and took it out to where I'd told her to sit – with her back to the sea and the clifftop twenty yards beyond. I poured the chilled white wine into the glass goblets. Dusk closed in as we ate. The candles blew out in the wind and the full moon shone down on us, bathing Jodie in silver.

Neither of us did more than nibble. Despite her attempts to beat me to it, I gathered the dishes, piled them. I stood there gripping the dirty plates and cutlery and said the words I'd held within for the last half an hour.

"When I return, we will talk. You…may talk."

The moon had risen enough that I could see how still she was, but with one hand she toyed with the white tablecloth, and with the other she turned her goblet like jerky clockwork.

When I returned, she remained mute. The chair under me crunched and settled in the sandy soil as I shifted my weight.

"You can talk," I said again, enunciating the words carefully, hoping she'd find something to say. Though her lips moved, she merely stared at the table then at me, as if I were something new and terrifying.

The answer dawned on me. I'd imagined this experience had forged a soul-deep bond between us.

But, this situation was so foreign, so out-there, that once exposed in the real world, it would shatter. I knew her from many past conversations, and she knew me. I could list how she took her coffee, what she liked doing on days off, her favorite sport and movies. And she could do the same for me. Yet we hadn't conversed for a month. I'd made myself her Master and her my slave and that had made us both strangers to each other despite our profound intimacy.

There must be a way to bridge the gap? Discussing the documentary would be so *so* wrong. Tomorrow, daytime, business-time, for that. This and now was personal.

I'd delved into, gloried in, my fantasies more than hers. I'd never asked her what she wanted since that first day.

"Jodie." I waited.

"Yes?"

"I want to know your fantasies. Tell me. Apart from your capture fantasies."

She made a small noise and shrugged in a way that spoke of uncertainty. I took her hand, marveling again at the delicacy of her bones and muscles when contrasted with mine. When she tried to pull away, I laid my other hand over the top. "Stay. Let me hold you." One last time? Perhaps.

I was scrambling for common ground. Tomorrow I might lose her. In the back of my head, a little part of me despaired. The contact of skin on skin calmed me though, and her too perhaps? Her shoulders lowered and she focused on how I enfolded her hand.

The worn groove of our Master-and-slave arrangement was proving difficult for both of us to escape from.

"Tell me. Tell me, now. "

"Do I have to?" So quiet.

"Yes."

"Oh." She pouted then sucked in a deep breath. I wanted to shake her to get her to answer. I was good. I waited, and I waited, stroking her hand.

"Okay." Then she continued on in a quiet voice. "I guess apart from my capture fantasies I've always liked the idea of being tied up and at someone's mercy."

"That, we've done." Not, *I've done to you*. I was learning. Back to the real.

"Mmm."

"More?" I wondered, hoping to hear that she'd always dreamed of being flogged or spanked. "What else?"

"I guess, I suppose, if you're looking for one that's different..."

"I am."

"Okay, well, I used to dream of being taken by more than one person, of being shared. Even of being made to. It's just...hot." She shook her head. "Stupid. No one does that." Her voice caught on the last word. Our eyes met.

Laughable. After our month of debauchery, she could still say that?

"You think? Men or women?"

Another long pause. A very long one interspersed with much screwing up of mouth and eyebrows. This question was agonizing to her. Cute though. "Both? Maybe? I guess?"

Ah. Now that *was* hot. "Sometimes people do the things that no one seems to do."

Like the light of morning lining the horizon, I realized, this could be my solution.

Kink was alive and well, and I knew just where to get it. This was something that bridged that gap. I could let her explore, join her in this, and show yet again how this fascinated us both. Was this going too far? I pulled out my phone and held it hard enough to hurt my bones. No, it wasn't. I'd have to be careful, though. Doing anything in public daunted me too. Things could go wrong. I only knew Moghul.

Would anyone there know us?

Damn. Stop stalling.

I sent a text, then waited for the reply, gave Moghul some more details in the next one. I sent another to Jon to check the whereabouts of his boat. Done. All good.

"We're going to a party."

"What?" A frown worked its way onto her forehead.

For this to work properly, I needed Jodie thinking as my slave yet again. If my subconscious laughed at my recent vow for that about-face, I smothered it. *One last time.*

Because maybe, if I showed her this was a two-way thing, that I could accommodate her needs too, she'd stay.

But that dress would never do, not as it was.

"Sit up straighter, Jodie, so I can see you."

"What?"

I added sternness. "Now." She blinked. I waited. Though she took longer than I'd have allowed her to without punishment a few days before, I let it go.

Finally, after one tremulous breath and a small amount of lip gnawing, she complied.

"Undo enough buttons so you can tuck the neckline under your breasts. Take off your bra. Cup your breasts so I can see them."

I stood, picking up and moving back the chair. While she undid the buttons, I took away the goblets and made the table top bare.

With the bodice opened enough, she put her hands under her breasts and lifted them, offering them to me. Bare breasted, areola showing against her pale skin, apart from that, Jodie was the picture of elegance. Mine to command. Heady. I zinged into Master mode like I'd never left.

I'd make that dress shorter. When we arrived, I'd bare her breasts like this and decorate her with the diamante nipple clamps and, I stepped behind the chair, there were more possibilities.

"Get up and lean over the table."

Oh yes. Like a good little doll, she draped her upper body over the table.

I took away her chair and I lifted the dress, rucked it up, slow, inch by inch. This was as heady as a slug of whiskey, revealing her intimate parts when she was dressed up and demure. White was innocence personified. I bared her whole ass and admired the contrast of white panties against skin. My lust barged in all impatient and almost throttled me.

"Whoa," I whispered. Her little moan spurred me on.

"Klaus –" she gasped out.

"Shh."

I'd missed doing this.

I wriggled her panties down her thighs so just the line of her sex showed and then clawed my fingers into her ass cheeks and separated them, thrilling at her whimpers. I'd been getting her ready for anal, but I hadn't done it yet. The medium plug at the party for starters. Yes. Then the biggest. Then me. Then perhaps whoever Moghul said was safe and who wanted to take her.

"Stay."

After wetting my finger with her slippery moisture, I pressed my fingertip to the rosette of her anus. Anal finger-fucking by moonlight. I smiled. It almost sounded romantic. I rotated my finger a little as I pushed it into her. After one squeak, she opened up more, groaning as I went in deeper, to the second knuckle.

With my finger still imbedded in her, I stepped back. The view was enough to turn my cock rock-hard. Jodie, ass-up over the table, dress flipped up and at the first stage of preparation for anal sex. I'd wanted this for so… Fucking. Long. I screwed my finger in farther, thrilling at her gasp and how she lifted herself into the thrust.

Lucky the neighbors couldn't see. A woman's derriere, as the French called it, was the best thing in nature. From the small of her back, to the subtle swell of her ass and the way it dipped down to the hollow at the juncture of her legs – so inviting. Even more so when my hand was buried there, when I could feel the heat and squeeze of her anal muscles and hear her gentle moans and trembles. The moment simmered. I leaned in, put my mouth to the dimple of her back, and kissed her.

What would it be like to watch another man fuck her? I knew it was something she wanted.

At the party, maybe I could do some spanking, hurt her a little if she seemed to like that too? This was my chance to cater to what she wanted. To find where we truly clicked.

Lightning hit. Holy crap. I was so stupid. When we'd started this weeks and weeks ago, when I'd had that epiphany about her documentary and told her how stupid she was, I'd listed all the things an evil man might do to her. This, sharing her with the man down the street, had been the last on that list. It wasn't quite the same, but damn near it. I had a feeling I'd gone and done most of those in between too, except attaching her nipples to bolts in the ceiling. Oh, yeah. That one I'd seen in my head. Came close.

My subconscious must have been writing that impromptu list.

My new epiphany turned creepy cold. Sharing hadn't been last on the list, killing her and burying her on the beach had been it. *Christ.* Thank God, I wasn't that man, but it made me wonder who I had become. I doubted I could change back.

I shook my head. I wasn't him. That was the important thing.

I left her there and went to find scissors to cut her dress, and all the toys, and to scan the medical tests we'd both had done before starting all this shit then email them to Moghul.

I was careful, gentle, driving us down to get the key from Jon.

Hard to imagine how this would be to her when she hadn't left the house in a month. Her dress was shorter, ripped to mid-thigh length, but decent. The buttons were done up again.

Streetlights weren't common but some glimpses of the set of her mouth, and the stiffness of her posture made me think she might be worried.

"It'll be okay. I'm going to go with the flow. See what you like. What I like. I'll keep you safe. Okay?"

I glanced across.

"Okay." She nodded and graced me with a small smile.

When I could, between changing gears I reached over and put a reassuring hand on her thigh. A few times, she sought out my hand with hers and wriggled her fingers under mine.

Though I had a general invite to use Jon's speed boat if he wasn't, the hour was late. I waited at the door and got an inquisitive lift of the eyebrow when he returned with the key. He spotted Jodie in the jeep.

"I see. You're back together? Have fun, man." He tossed me the keys.

I shrugged. "Will do. Thanks."

So odd. An old friend here, and a girlfriend in the car who'd let me enslave her for a month. This was a scene from the *Twilight Zone*.

The sea was flat. Wind speed barely a few knots. We made the trip across to the mainland in twenty minutes. The taxi I'd ordered took us to the house where the party was on.

At the end of a long concrete driveway, a modern house was lit up, all angles and large plate glass windows. The tops of palm trees were silhouetted against the pale gray sky. There was no loud music, just fifteen or so cars parked along the street. Somewhere in the darkness nearby, water tinkled, as if from a fountain.

Jodie seemed shell-shocked that the driver had spoken to her. With the bottom of her dress torn off like it was, the man had almost had his tongue on the floor when we got into his car.

She clutched at the cloth of her dress. Nervous?

Her eyes were dark, darker than even the night around us. Fear? Well, I had that too. I buried mine by taking hold of her hand. This was her fantasy I was doing. For her.

Wrong. Fool. Face it, this was more for me. For a whole month I'd let myself just *be*. Once I'd gotten my head around the idea that I could live my out my desires, I had. I'd done what I wanted to with Jodie, like a child running around with a new damn toy. I had avoided thinking about the end as much as I could. I'd been obscenely one-way, one-track, one *everything*. I'd dreamed this wouldn't end. Now I was up shit creek without a paddle, in so deep I needed a snorkel, and a lot of other really bad analogies.

I shut my eyes and felt the soft lightness of her hand in mine. Despite it all, maybe she trusted me. Yeah? Why, though? That was the crux of it. I didn't know why she should still trust me. I didn't understand her, or me, or any goddamned thing. The end result was all I could comprehend. You are mine. Full stop.

I had a sudden urge to do like I had that day when I taught her how to rescue herself if she was upside down in a kayak – just before I deliberately flipped it over so she was underwater. Trust me, I'd asked her. When was I going to be brave enough to say that again?

I could see myself going down on one knee and asking that. *Trust me.*

No ring, no marriage proposal, just those words. Okay, maybe a collar. I liked her with my collar on. Putting a proper ownership one on her neck would be incredibly satisfying. I'd be ten feet tall with my eyes on fire.

But me, the one kneeling? After all I'd taught her? That would look bad. Total power exchange. TPE. I'd figured out that's what I needed…wanted. Either that or something so illegal I'd be put away for a hundred years. Kneeling was not an option. Leastways it wasn't in the rules I'd read.

Enough maudlin regrets. Enough fucking diddling about. Time to go.

After this, after I showed her she could trust me, then I'd make sure we had a talk. Bridge the gap between the fantasy of the last month and the reality. Then talk.

"Okay," I muttered. "When the going gets tough the tough get kinky."

She swung her head. "What?"

On the way over Moghul had sent another text. There was one couple interested, up there, inside that house.

"Come." I hefted the overnight bag with my toys, then tugged, and led her up the driveway. For once, I figured I was as on edge as she was. This had to work, because if it failed I'd be lost.

Moghul met us at the door. Just inside was a small square timber table. This place was big enough for a two-story-high foyer. The low bass of music thumped from the living room beyond, where people sat on couches and chatted. From the quick check I made, my jeans and shirt would pass for a Dom, but Jodie was over-dressed. Black leather harnesses, collars, leashes, pretty corsets and even some kitty costumes were worn by the men and women who sat on the floor or in the laps of those I assumed were their dominants. A woman in a pink micro-mini was getting loudly spanked to everyone's amusement.

Moghul, though…

I'd only seen the present-day Moghul from his Fetlife pics which didn't show his face properly. Though he'd obviously done well for himself over the past five years, the man looked like a dressed-up Hells Angel biker – tattooed biceps, thick brown hair shorn in a ragged fashion, stubble, faded jeans and T-shirt.

"How's it going, Klaus. Long time no see." He smiled as he held out his hand but I could see him assessing me. "Good that you made it. This is Jodie?"

I glanced across at her. You wouldn't know this was the feisty self-made woman from a month ago. She stood near my shoulder and seemed to be one second away from leaning into me. For comfort? I could see the worry radiating from her. On impulse, I put my arm around her shoulders, tucking her into my body. The surge of warmth I got from that pleased me. I liked holding her like this too. I'd forgotten, in a way, how important simple skin contact, just touching, could be.

"Yes, this is Jodie." The scent of her hair a few inches away made me want to kiss her.

"Wait." He ducked back a few feet, and put his head around the door as if searching for someone.

I'd seen the party rules weeks ago, and there they were taped on the small table.

Play at your own risk.

No street clothes once through the door. Submissives dressed as submissives. Kinky fetish shit is encouraged. No playing with others unless you have express permission. All extreme play – blood, scat, water sports, rape play and anything else you think could bother others MUST be cleared by the Dungeon Masters – Moghul or Steve. House safeword is red or safeword. Any transgressors will be most likely be asked to leave immediately.

No alcohol or drugs.

Have fun but play safe.

Moghul called out, "Steve, man the perimeter for a while, please. Good? Thanks." On his return, he asked us to follow him and led us across the living room past the small crowd and into a study. He perched his hip on the corner of a steel-and-glass desk, wrapped his hand over the edge, and regarded us quietly.

"Okay. Even though I know you, Klaus, we have things to discuss. This is the first play party for both of you? Yes? And I need to talk to Jodie. Since she's your submissive, I'm asking you first. So, is that okay?"

Questions? Jesus.

"Yes. It's okay."

What the hell would she say?

I really did not know. But to get things on the right footing...

I signaled to her. "Kneel."

Strange, the relief when she obeyed.

"Now you can ask her."

∽ *Chapter Nineteen* ∾

Jodie

I looked up at this man, this friend of Klaus's. He seemed kind, if imposing, plus, yes, a little scary in some odd way, as if he might be more than willing to punish anyone breaking his party rules. Those brown eyes were honest, but no-nonsense. I knew the look now. Klaus had given off that same aura, ever since we started this whole strange adventure.

The carpet was raw on my knees. When I shifted in discomfort, without hesitation, Moghul raised an eyebrow and said, "Floor too hard?"

I nodded.

He walked to the window seat which was covered in pretty cushions, gently moved aside a cream Persian cat, and sorted through the cushions.

Here I was, kneeling before two men, being treated as something lesser. I didn't even consider protesting.

Klaus. I shivered a little. I liked, plain fucking liked, being his. I felt safer than ever before. I was wrapped in his persona. If he gave me pain, I liked it anyway because somehow that reasserted his authority, and it said, *I want you.* Every pain, every wind of rope, every snap of the cane wrote, *mine*, in bold red letters on my skin and in my mind. And the needles, holy shit, though they'd seared me when they went in, and sent pain lancing through me while I lay there bound, I'd still loved it, all of it.

Pain and pleasure and possession had become inextricably wound together.

I wasn't sure what date it was today. But from the recent changes, I thought this was a Sunday – the last Sunday. I could sense Klaus was uncertain, and because of that, so was I. Where would we go from here?

I knew it was a little crazy, but I dreaded this ending. I hadn't stayed with him because he forced me. His new forcefulness was what made me *want* to stay. I could have spoken. I could. Yet what we had wasn't sustainable. I existed in a kinky la-la fluffy land, below the storms, beneath the waves of the insane real world. I was leaning on him way too much.

But…*sigh*…I didn't know how to stop. We'd been in so deep.

Tonight, this was us, surfacing, and seeing if we could breathe again, together.

Moghul returned with a flat cushion. "Can I give her this?" Klaus nodded, and Moghul tossed it to me.

I didn't thank him. I knew better. Klaus hadn't said not to speak, but in here his rules from the past month had somehow fallen back into place in my head. From how he acted, he thought the same, and I wanted to please him. I edged my knees up onto the cushion.

I listened carefully, brushing aside my thoughts. Missing some new rule might be dangerous in this house full of kinky people. And, though I'd learned to like some danger, I wasn't stupid.

"Okay." He resumed his seat on the desk, and looked at us both. "I know from Klaus that you've only been exploring kink for a month or so. All of those here are longtime friends in the lifestyle. The only way you get in is if I know you well. I know you, Klaus. You're sensible. But both of you need to be careful you're not going too far. Even Doms can go past their limits. I don't care about your kinks as long as you stick to the rules and play consensually and safely. But Jodie has to remember the safeword is there if she needs it." He nodded at me. "And you, Klaus, have to both watch her for problems as well as yourself. Don't hesitate to stop everything and ask for advice. That includes me and Steve, or Damien the other Dom. So. Good?"

I nodded and Klaus said, "Sure."

"Also a general rule is that if you play sexually or with body fluids outside your normal partner you use condoms, even though we've all been tested. It's common sense. You'll find Damien will stick to that, and expect you to also." Moghul stood. "Take care and have fun tonight. There's non-alcoholic drinks and snacks available. I've got you a room to play in. Private is better this time?"

Panicked, I glanced at Klaus, but he barely acknowledged Moghul's unspoken invitation to do this in public.

"Okay. Room it is. Any questions?"

When I made a small noise, and rested my gaze on him, Klaus gave a nudge with his chin. Permission. Relief swept me.

I took a breath. "Can we wear masks? Something." I dropped my voice. "I don't want to be recognized."

"No, you can't. And there are others here who are well known in the community. Unless it's fancy dress, we don't conceal our faces. You'd make yourself the outsiders. If you're not happy with that, you can't stay."

I put my teeth on my lower lip. Panic fluttered in my chest. Here I was admitting that I was a well-known person. By mentioning my concerns, I felt as if I'd stuck up my head and shouted out, *here I am. Here I am. Look at me.* I wanted to hide again. Klaus stepped closer and put his palm on my head. Without thinking, I leaned toward him and found his trouser leg beside my face. I inhaled. Calm floated back in.

Funny how he'd known. We were like two peas in a pod. Psychic twins. I could tell he liked this, that he was glad he could reassure me.

Maybe this could work.

If he'd just wanted to hurt me, I would have run away long ago.

"Would you like to mingle first or go upstairs?"

"Upstairs," Klaus said without hesitation.

Where anything could happen. Performing on stage paled against this – on a scale of one to ten this was a million and on stage was ten at most. Upstairs might be heaven or hell, or even worse, it might fall flat as a pancake. But Klaus wanted me to try. My palms sweated, and cold goose bumps rose all along my arms and the back of my neck.

"She's not really dressed correctly."

Oh. Guess I wasn't. I looked down at the dress and the row of tiny buttons. Slight cleavage showed, but apart from the torn hem, I was normal.

"No. But it fits the way I want her to look. Though only at the beginning. I want her innocent yet fuckable."

At that Moghul turned and really examined me. After a second, I dropped my gaze to the rug, and waited.

Fuckable. Said so casually, it was thrilling what that single word had done. I nearly shuddered at the delicious dirty feeling coursing through me.

"Yeah. I get that. Kneeling there in that white dress, she looks like she's been in a nunnery for most of her life. I'd like to strip her too. Just make sure when she leaves the room she's showing more flesh. Come on. Let's go meet Damien and his sub, Kat."

The blatant male assessment of my body, awakened me. My nipples stood to attention and rubbed on the fabric as I stood. No bra, so everything wobbled when I moved – the penalties of being full-breasted.

I followed, walking again past the crowd, trying to be small and unnoticed and simply the submissive who followed Klaus. This seemed as surreal as the last month. How had I ended up here? And who was waiting for us upstairs? What would they do to me? Klaus hadn't discussed a thing. That was normal for us, but here? No.

Yet again, I liked that he hadn't asked what I wanted, but it scared me too. Having sex with another man, another woman, not normal at all. But...I watched the steps as we ascended...it aroused me. God. This could be amazing.

Feminine squeals and the smacking sound of hand on flesh echoed from somewhere above.

Upstairs was a balcony overlooking below and a small lounge with a huge square window that showed blackness, a hallway with four rooms, and from the glimpse through a doorway, a bathroom. This wasn't a small or cheap house. I didn't know what Moghul did for a living, but he had a lot more money than I did. Oodles more. We went to the end door. Inside was a huge king-size bed, a door that might lead to an en-suite bathroom, and a low square table with two tan leather sofas in an L-shape. A breeze blew in, rattling the propped-open French doors and blowing the cream curtain into the room. Though Moghul stepped over and shut the doors, what really grabbed my attention were the man and woman on one of the sofas.

"Damien, Kat, this is Klaus and his submissive, Jodie." By the time they'd nodded back, Moghul was at the door. I heard it click shut.

She, a cute blonde with bright pink streaks, was draped across his lap with her ass glowing nicely red. I knew who'd been squealing. Kat. Her hair was in pigtails and her figure curvaceous. I'd never had any trouble admiring women and the thought we might do something to each other already had me buzzing. Like many of the Doms, Damien was dressed in jeans and shirt; his shirt was pastel orange, of all things. Kat had on a black corset with cherries on it, lacy stockings and garters plus that bright red hand print on one butt cheek to match the cherries.

"Klaus." The accent was European for sure. And Damien's cropped blond hair bore that out. He had a Scandinavian look to him. A neat, strong-featured man.

Only Klaus had got that nod from Damien. Something told me I was the least person in this room – at the bottom of the pecking order and about to be pecked. From beside me I heard Klaus inhale deeply.

"Hi. Kat is your submissive?"

Huh. Obvious. The woman did have the handprint from the spanking.

"Most of the time, yes. Sometimes, we switch. And…" Damien eyed me. "She loves topping other women. Even gets quite into the S and m. You good with that? All of us domming Jodie?"

"Sure," Klaus replied.

What? I snapped a glance at him. That expression – slightly fearsome, and he saw me looking and lifted one corner of his mouth as he returned the stare. Already I could tell he was thinking of devious things. A shiver took me. I squeezed closed my eyes then was shocked by his big hand grabbing the back of my neck.

"Keep your eyes and mouth shut," he whispered harshly right in my ear. His hot breath coasted over my skin, sending a shiver down my neck.

God. Klaus had stepped into his Master persona. His bag of toys smacked to the floor.

"Come outside on the balcony so we can talk." That was to Damien. "But first." His hand forced me to kneel and I hit the carpet with my hands to stop my fall. He growled to me. "Put your wrists crossed over at your back." I did so, aware of my breasts arching outward. "Stay."

"Can Kat touch her?" Damien's voice.

"Sure. Whatever she wants. No undressing though. We can keep an eye on them. Let's talk about what you'd like to do to her."

Fuck. *To me.* I got so wet so suddenly it shocked me.

I was perversely proud that Klaus, the newcomer, had taken charge. But then Damien was a switch, a sometimes submissive. Did that make him weaker? I didn't know, but he was no match for my Master.

The slide of a body on leather then feet padding on carpet warned me Kat approached.

So vulnerable – not seeing. I almost turned to look but… *Eyes closed, remember?* I didn't want to disobey Klaus.

"Hi there, sweetie." Her silky voice glided smooth as syrup from behind me.

Something about the tone of it pricked me awake. *Danger.*

I felt her hand in the middle of my back – small compared to Klaus and gentle, barely noticeable. For a while she was just there, stroking me, feeling me all over, down over the mounds of my ass, around my waist and then all over my back again. Relaxing yet arousing.

She continued softly, "We can be friends later. I'm nice when you get to know me, but I'm not when I'm in Dommy mode, not when I have a girl like this. You know. Fresh meat."

I shuddered, felt the early swell of lust.

"You're new, aren't you? I promise I can be careful. We'll see what your Dom will let us do. Damien and I are sooo grateful you two came along. Now tonight will be way more fun."

She moved both her hands to my shoulders then her chin rested near the angle of neck and shoulder. Her tongue slowly licked my ear lobe for a few strokes before she sucked it into her mouth and nibbled. Warm, and with her moist little breath huffing in my ear, I wanted to squirm.

I'd never even been touched by a woman before, not in this sexual way, but having her touch me and also want to do things to me, like Klaus…it sent me soaring.

"You know we're all going to dominate you. Damien will Dom me, but tonight, you are ours." Her knee and thigh edged between my legs and pushed into me.

Jesus. I could nearly come from the idea alone. I rocked into her thigh, letting out a soft, barely-there groan.

"You like?" Kat laughed and licked my ear once. The soft play turned into a hard bite at the same time as she snaked her arms around me. One arm, set below my breasts like a bar, pulled me to her. With her other hand she found my breast, and pinched. Her finger and thumb hit my nipple dead center.

The needle trauma from three days ago arced into prominence – pain screwed in. I squealed and automatically swept my hands around to grab at her.

"Stop!" A deep, gnarly voice that vibrated with force – Klaus.

I froze, caught in a riptide of emotions. Fear. Excitement. Anticipation. And my clit throbbed. I couldn't deny that. I had a hate-love relationship with Klaus and his punishments. I hadn't heard them come back. From the sound and close scent of him, he'd squatted before me.

"Open your eyes."

I did, staring unblinking into his, and at the sculpted line of his lips as he spoke.

"Did you do bad?"

"Yes, Sir. I'm sorry."

"Say that to Kat."

Kat, who'd let go of my nipple when Klaus snapped at me. I grinned inside, amused he'd done that to her. I'd bet he scared her too.

I inclined my head so I could glimpse her. "I'm sorry I moved, Kat." And I was. But I wasn't. But I was. Fuck. Messed up. If I was this bad already, what would the rest of the night hold?

Her breasts moved against my back as she inhaled. "That's okay, darling, I'll make you pay later."

"Now, bad girl." Klaus deliberately reached in very slowly and, while spearing me with his gaze, took hold of both my nipples through the cloth. "Up."

The pain screeched into molten but I only hissed and scrambled to my feet. He released my nipples, leaving them pulsing, aching. The muscles of his face stirred, and that harsh mask he wore when he wanted to hurt me flickered, and went away. "Good?" he ground out.

He was asking? Was he asking if I was good, as in okay?

I poised there, stunned, swaying. I'd never seen this before, not in the middle of a scene. The sadistic Klaus was always *on* during play. I summoned a nod.

Like storm clouds covering the sky, *He* returned, and Klaus moved back a step, then circled behind me. "Arms by your sides, Jodie."

"She's well trained for only a month." Damien had been a step behind Klaus. His hands rested casually on his hips, making his shirt stretch across his chest and his biceps stand out. He had muscles, but I was sure Klaus could take him easily.

Eh. I had this odd need to see Klaus as the best. I guess I was proud of him. I guess…because he was mine, the same as I was his.

Damn.

That was it. I'd been so blind. All I needed was to find a place we were both happy. I was abruptly ice-blindingly clear on that. This, tonight, was his way of finding that place. He knew, like I did, that we needed each other now. Interdependent. Not just me as his. Klaus was mine. My Dom, my Master. Mine.

He'd said long ago that all I wanted was to fuck him. He'd been right. I'd kept my distance from really being with him, fended him off with excuses. Now, we had more. Not just S and m and kink, but a way of feeling, of *being*, that matched. I would kiss the very ground he walked on to be with *him*.

And he felt the same. I was certain.

But really, we had this now. It wasn't a matter of finding. We had it. We only needed to fine tune. When this was done, I would kneel at his feet and tell him so. Men were sometimes stupid. I would tell him and we'd sort this out slowly. We'd get there in the end.

Tears welled. I blinked them back.

"Well-trained? Yes, she is. I'm going to present her to you. If you could both sit on the couch?"

"Course I can." Kat strolled to the couch Damien had chosen, turned quickly, and flopped back into it. After flicking her pigtails aside, Damien draped his arm around her, over her neck. She toyed with his fingers while smiling at me, predatory-like.

The woman had balls. I was riveted. Her and Klaus seemed even chances for planning evilness tonight.

"You'd better watch her," Klaus said quietly to me. "I will be."

Before he could say more, Kat growled out a question. "What can I do to her, Sir?" That was a feminine, kitty cat growl – one that had crawled up my spine and heated me, and scared me too.

"I want to eat her all up." She blatantly studied my lower half. "I want to make her eat me. I want to spank her and other things, and I really want watch you two fuck her."

Damien chuckled. "Hell, woman. You're no sub tonight."

"For you I am, Sir." She kissed his hand. "But for her I'm all Domme."

I swallowed. I wasn't allowed to answer her. And if I had been, I would've stayed mute.

"I'll watch you, Kat. I'll stop you if you go too far. Now, let's get started." Klaus murmured.

He shifted the big square coffee table away. Then, with his hand at my back he urged me forward until I stood before the two of them. The bright look in Kat's eyes and the slow lick of her tongue across her lips made me think of a kid about to get an ice cream.

Damien smirked. "How about you tie her hands together since she can't keep them down? I want to be able to get at her without being clawed."

"Good suggestion."

While I watched nervously, Klaus unpacked a heap of gear from his bag and laid everything in a row. With the cuffs and my collar in hand, he came back.

"Not using rope?" Damien sat forward. "I like rope. It looks good against women's skin."

While he fastened the cuffs to my ankles, Klaus replied, "No. I like these. Easy to get off in a hurry. In case..." He held my ankle in his fist a moment, warm, firm, and *mmm*, good. My pussy clenched. "In case something happens."

"Yeah, I get that. It's safer and quicker, but I still like my rope. You should come to a class sometime." Damien patted Kat's shoulder. "Kat likes rope too, on her. Says it makes her feel more held down."

"Yeah, it's good." She was watching Klaus work at putting all the leather on me. "But this is good too."

The collar was fastened and buckled. I shut my eyes and breathed. *Oh. Yes.*

Amusement colored Kat's voice. "The collar, she likes that a lot. I can see it on her face." She leaned toward me and whispered, "I'll bet that got you wet, girl."

"How about you find out." Klaus pulled my hands behind me and clipped my wrists together. He made me shuffle closer, closer. I resisted a little, scuffing my feet. This was like entering a dragon's cave.

"Don't be shy. This is what you want." Kat bit her lip – such square white teeth – I couldn't look away. "You want us to make you do the naughtiest things. Come to me."

Damien watched her and me, fascinated, and terribly amused. I could see his cock straining at his pants. Another man, another woman. *Frick.*

A soft kiss on my neck stirred goose bumps to life all down my arms. "Isn't she a little picture of purity, Kat, Damien. All in white, with just a torn dress to say maybe there's more to her. I'll hold her still." His words pattered out like falling rain. I listened to the warm timbre, inches away, coaxing, mesmerizing me. He gripped my arms at the elbow, and made me take that last step.

"That's it. Good girl." Smiling, and careful as a horse trainer gentling a new filly, Kat reached out and touched inside my knee then trailed her fingers upward, upward. With her other hand she inched the dress up my thighs until she had it pushed to crotch level. Then she slid her hand between my legs.

I stopped breathing. I'm sure my eyes widened and I definitely quivered. Heat rushed down there.

"Ooo. Look at that blush. Wow, sweetie, this is early days too. The shit we are going to do to you." Kat stroked a finger, up and down my cleft. "She is sweet. God, I'm getting so hot looking at you, feeling your pussy."

"Put your finger inside her and lick her." Damien urged Kat forward then leaned his elbows on his knees.

"In my own time. I'm in no hurry. Who wants to hurry a gourmet meal? Well?" She addressed me. "Do you want my tongue on you, in you? Hmm? I can do amazing things to girls."

I was starting to believe that.

Up and down, then around my clit her finger was going, round and round, brushing me, tantalizing. And speaking of tongues, the tip of hers emerged and cruised wetly along her lip as she concentrated on my face. I don't think she realized, but I did. I watched her moist flicking tongue, and she fiddled with me down there more.

I choked out a small noise when she ran that finger straight over that little sexual button. *Press me, turn me on.* My eyelids fluttered lower. My thighs squeezed on her hand. If she kept up that dirty talk while playing with me I was going to come.

"Let's show them some more of you." Klaus let go of my elbows and smoothed his hands around me until he reached my breasts. There was Kat, playing, keeping me on the boil so bad I was thrusting onto her hand just a tiny amount, and now Klaus undid all my buttons to my waist, and pulled the neckline of the dress down, exposing my breasts.

Gently, he circled my nipples, and tugged on them. I groaned. One of them circling my clit, Klaus leaning over me, watching his own hands, and Kat staring up, also watching.

"She's going to come soon." The couch creaked. Damien stood.

"Is she?" Kat asked, smiling. "That's my girl. Show me what you do when you come."

My breathing had turned to pants, my thighs strained forward. *Touch me.* I wanted her fingers to do more, just a little, more.

I hadn't seen him come closer, but Damien was there beside me, crouching.

"Suck on her." Klaus took his hand away and Damien instead took hold, gripping my breast rather than cupping it. His hand was calloused. While I was processing how all of them were playing with a different part of me, he lowered his head and drew my nipple into the hot cavern of his mouth.

"Oh." I gasped and held my breath, looking down. I felt my panties drawn down my legs. Kat slipped her fingers straight up inside me, spearing in, slowly fucking me with them. I parted my legs as much as I could, feeling her hands dragging against my inner thighs as she thrust into me.

The liquid craving of an orgasm pumped higher with each drive of her fingers and each suck of Damien's mouth. Klaus tugged on my other nipple. Muscles tensed. The awesome constriction at my wrists, fed into the maelstrom. Sensations circled, whirling.

"Now," Kat murmured from below. "You're there. You're there, sweetheart. Show me how you come."

Enthralled, I saw her move, and she put her mouth onto me, covered my clit in that warm wetness and dragged her tongue up and over. Soft, firm, fucking hot.

I arched, and cried out, open-mouthed, ripping molten and seething into the little explosion of an orgasm. My thighs tightened and I leaned back into Klaus as pleasure rippled outward from where she'd buried her mouth. Her continued sucking trapped me there, rapt in the sensations of the climax.

While I was barely aware, before I could register another thought, Klaus pulled my panties off, and made me stumble to the end of the couch where he bent me ass-up over the arm.

I was still quivering from coming when he began to slam his hand onto my ass. No preamble, no preparation, I cried a little at the first then mewed some more with each following blow. Damien grabbed my hair and laughed at my wriggling and noises. The couch shifted and creaked and I thought I saw Kat go by. There was a pause in the blows. A small hand caressed my burning skin then parted the cheeks of my ass. Coldness drizzled on me. I knew what that meant and pulled on my wrist cuffs then twisted, trying to get up. It was instinctive, I knew it wouldn't work, but I tried.

"Oh no." Kat had that smile in her tone. "You're not getting away, pretty thing. You got her Damien?"

"Sure have." His hand screwed tighter in my hair. "Do what you want back there."

Uh. I sagged, surrendering, onto the couch. Nothing I could do.

The hard tip of a butt plug pressed on my other hole and started to slide in by tiny increments. More pushing in, more pulsing, and I groaned at the intolerable burn.

"Push out. Relax, Jodie." Klaus. My man. "Talk. Swear if you want to."

Uh. He liked hearing me protest sometimes. I wouldn't. Not this time. I hissed and whined at the hurt, but I tried to relax, and I guess it helped. The thing slid farther until I thought it could go no deeper. *No. Hell. No fricking more.* With me squealing *fuck fuck fuck* out loud after all, it slipped past the rim and into me. Done. The strange feel of crazy bursting pain changed into the heat of pleasure and I moaned into the fabric of the couch.

So vulnerable, so trapped. The three of them were all over me and I was bound as well.

"Damn, I liked that when she squeaked." Kat slipped her fingers along in the moisture on my pussy, and toyed with my poor clit. I grunted and pushed up onto my toes. I hated *hated* that when I'd just come. But they held me down and though I panted and writhed at her touch, my clit hummed back to life.

After an experimental single swish that I recognized as a crop slicing the air, she began to crop my rear. Only the flat leather end never got used except on my engorged clit. It was the whippy shaft slamming in on my butt, and tapping on me softly, sometimes on the butt plug, before smacking in again on my flesh.

I knew it was Kat because Klaus had come around to squat near my head. He watched, nothing more, eyes as distant as the stars, absorbing my cries and gasps of pain, my whimpers of pleasure.

"She's in love with your ass," he said quietly to me during a break from the exquisite song of pain and pleasure. He swept strands of hair from before my eyes, tucked them behind my ear. "I think she'd take it home with her if she could."

I smiled at him. *Silly.*

At that, I felt Kat nuzzle in between my thighs and find my clit again. God, she knew what to do there. I parted my legs, letting her in. Her tongue might be smaller than Klaus's but she used it expertly, taking me to the brink of another orgasm.

I was filled tight with that aching pressure. I groaned and tried to hump the couch, hearing Kat laugh as I did so. She used her hand on me again then her mouth, then the crop. The pain held me in transit. Too hard. She was deliberately torturing me and not allowing me to come.

"Make her make me come, Sir, please," I begged.

Klaus smiled and kissed me awhile, probing at my lips with his tongue, until I opened and let him in. He put his forehead to mine. "She will, but I'm going to fuck your ass now. While I do, I want you to suck off Damien. It will please me. Okay?"

"Yes," I gasped, for Kat was at me again, I tilted back my hips to give her more access, hoping for relief, but she only took my clit between her teeth and bit until I screamed, then bit all along my thighs.

"Wow. You've got her all stirred up." Damien seemed amazed. "She's a biter though. I have the scars to prove it."

"No scars, Kat. Don't bite like that," Klaus snapped as he rose to his feet.

"No, Sir, I won't. I'm only teasing her."

"Good."

A pause then Kat spoke up, "You know the safeword, Jodie?"

"Uh-huh." My throat was thick. I squirmed. My heartbeat thudded down the scale from gallop to fast thud.

"Say it," she insisted.

What? Oh. A command. I managed to choke out that one word. "Safeword."

I closed my eyes to feel the sensations better, *he* was going back there. I felt the suction and discomfort as the butt plug was removed, flinched once, then the probe as Klaus put his cock to me, and pushed...in.

Oh fuck. I put my head down and panted through it.

In, farther in, and the slide of his cock burned and throbbed at me. I felt myself opening more and more. And yet I was tight enough that it stung.

I liked it, hated it, and felt the oncoming wave of an orgasm reassembling because someone was playing with my clit while he ass-fucked me. Kat, for sure.

"No. No. No," I whimpered, arching back into Klaus as I did so. And then he was in, all the way. His body pressed on me back there. For a while he stayed there, deep, leaning with his full bodyweight while my muscles readjusted.

A tongue, Kat's tongue, licked on my aching nub. I was so aroused it seemed engorged beyond belief. Big and tight, bursting. Lust swept me. Another lick from her as Klaus started to thrust in and out, a little quicker. I could tell when she curled her tongue over and when she flicked or dabbed.

"Unh." *More.* I writhed a bit, striving to put myself on her tongue just where it should be.

"You know the safeword, Jodie?" Damien was asking, maybe for the third time. Whatever, whoever, Damien thought he was, Dom or not, seemed like tonight he was letting Kat run wild.

I gasped again and nodded, not wanting to talk, to lose that thread that led to the ultimate pleasure. That thrust inside my ass, that lick of tongue...

A wrapper ripped and Damien grabbed my hair again to tilt back my head. I watched helpless as, one handed, he rolled a condom onto his cock. He slid over and shoved a pillow under my upper body.

"Suck it in." Then Damien fed the head into my mouth. I had three of them on me, again. Used. Fucked. The best. I hit the climax hard, spasming tight then almost convulsing, screaming silently.

I didn't bite Damien, but I found my mouth clamped onto his dick when I stopped coming.

"Jeez." He pulled me off by my hair then croaked. "Can you pull out, Klaus? I want her to sit on me while you fuck her."

Though trembling, I did as they wanted. With Kat watching avidly, perched cross-legged on the couch beside Damien, I was positioned over Damien's cock and made to slide down him. I groaned at the thickness stretching me down there, heard the slick sounds of my moisture lubricating the path as I was ever so slowly spitted on his cock. Down. Farther in. God.

My wrists were still caught behind me in the cuffs. As before, the knowledge that I could do nothing except perform for them and be their toy, thrilled me. My thighs trembled and I shut my eyes for a second and just *felt* that deep penetration.

"Almost. There. Damn, that's nice." The rasp in Damien's words betrayed his arousal.

He watched me take the last inch of him, swallowing and moaning as I did so. Then Klaus penetrated me again, gradually, until he was in balls deep. My legs were well spread. Both of them were inside. My knee touched Kat's. I couldn't do anything except breathe for a few seconds, head bowed, mouth open.

"Oh, that's it," she murmured. "The two of you inside the little bitch. Love it. Fucking love it. Hey, bruises." She reached up and touched my breast. "You've been needled there."

If she wanted an answer, she wasn't getting one, we were...preoccupied.

Damien had split me in a most intimate unstoppable way. I couldn't get off him without help, not with my hands at my back. Double penetration. God. I'd dreamed of this many times. I shuddered. From then on all he did was smile at my predicament and play with my breasts and nipples while Klaus thrust.

There was pain but also the throb of pleasure with the two men inside me at once. The incredible pressure of an orgasm built in my groin. But I realized this was for them. Their domination. Their pleasure.

For a few jabbing thrusts Klaus took me in a headlock and held me. Tight, so tight. I loved it when he possessed me, and anal was the ultimate domination of my body. With his head right close to mine, I felt the warmth of his exhalations. I knew he listened to the sounds I made. This was for him. I made sure to let him know that I was his and whimpered well each time he speared in.

With his cock jammed as deep as he could go, with no space between our bodies, and the echo of his breathing in my ear, he came in my ass. He kissed my neck and let me go. I collapsed, ending up with my face buried in Damien's shoulder, gasping. I hadn't come, but I was happy, sublime. I'd gone into that serene place that sometimes took me. Subspace.

This seemed a night for Klaus to observe. He mostly watched from then on while Kat took over and did whatever she wanted. I was stripped and strapped on my back to the square coffee table, hands above me, my feet on the floor and legs tied to the table legs. Kat and Damien put clamps on my nipples and then he came inside me, plowing me roughly, tugging on the clamps until I cried out. The table got shoved inches along the floor. From a distance, I heard the screeches.

I fuzzed in and out of subspace. At one point I wondered crazily if I might break. Or maybe Kat would have a heart attack. The woman was impressive, mad, and amazingly good at wringing climaxes from me. Her tongue could've won a gold medal for gymnastics.

An electric vibrator was plugged in and I was made to come again. I grew dizzy and lost count, and Klaus viewed every detail from the couch. I was so hazed that nothing could touch me. Or so I thought. Kat left the room, returned, and the needles arrived.

I watched bewildered from my splayed position as she talked to Klaus and he nodded. He rose to his feet and trod across the floor to me, squatted by my head, and gripped my wrists where they were somewhere behind my head. I blinked up at him. Beautiful gray eyes.

Another sound, more feet on the floor. Kat. The packet of needles swung in her gloved hand. She knelt and took hold of my breast.

Terror seized me. *No. No, no, no.* But I no longer knew words. I blinked, horrified. The paper was peeled back and the needle emerged. The needle was twisted and removed. *Cold.* She swiped something across me there. A tang flooded my nose. A sharp thing pricked my nipple.

I gasped. A needle. He was allowed those, not her. Not a stranger. I floated, aware yet lost. My heart cringed as I waited for the metal sting. The fear was there outside me. When the needle bit it would push in fear and agony and mix with my blood and I would *hurt*.

No.

She stopped and spoke. I blinked again, wetness on my lashes, barely hearing.

No.

A word was needed. But I mustn't use those. It was up to him. I turned my head to see him. I heard the rasp of my hair on the table. I pleaded with my eyes. *Hear me.* But the man in there was *Him*, the sadist, the distant one. He didn't know me anymore. He just watched.

As the needle found me, I was screaming, quietly *screaming*.

⁓ *Chapter Twenty* ⁓

Klaus

"Is she okay? Can she safeword? I can't get an answer from her." Kat's words barely penetrated the world I inhabited. That needle at Jodie's nipple, I wanted to see it go in, wanted to watch her writhe.

Without hesitating, I answered. "She's okay. Keep going."

I'd never drawn blood, not properly. The little needles barely showed a bleb. A bigger needle, like this, what would it do? I flicked a look at Jodie's face, ready to drink in whatever telltale signs she showed. Half the fun in this, the thrill, was seeing her reactions. If she bled, would that push her higher? It would me. I knew it would. My dick throbbed in anticipation. I didn't want to miss a single microsecond of this.

Blood. There was something primeval about the red stuff on the white landscape of skin.

Why wasn't Kat doing it?

"You're certain, Klaus? Klaus? Hey, I've had subs forget. And some won't say it. I don't know her like you do. I need to be certain."

Oh fuck. I blinked, dragged in a breath. *What was I doing?*

Jodie. I saw her eyes and the desperation. I saw the raw terror. Kat was looking at me, her hand wrapped around Jodie's breast, the needle between her fingers.

"Stop," I croaked as I lunged. I grasped Kat's wrist and pulled it upward. "Yes. She's safewording."

I'd crapped all over this. What was I doing? So wrong. So fucking wrong. An ache built to Armageddon level in my forehead. I'd said yes to this without thinking of anything but me.

"Let's get her untied. Now." My hands trembled for a second before I brought them under control. She needed me, but in the back of my mind a litany ran in a loop. *I fucked up.*

My last thought before I stopped this had been of seeing her blood. Her blood. When had she said yes to that? BDSM was consensual, right? Fool was too mild for me. I hadn't learned at all. Where was I going to stop? The imaginary man on that list who wanted to kill her, bury her on the beach? I swallowed. Maybe that was potentially me, a year down the track. Who the hell knew?

Not relevant right now. I ignored the devastation and the ugly collapse inside me. I needed to help her.

Kat comforted her as we peeled her off the table and laid her on the couch. They were good people underneath. Kinky but good. I was a fool. We dressed Jodie, wrapped her in blankets while they said words at me like *safeword* and *subspace* and *she needs some TLC.* I had to wipe my eyes once while I waited in the study for the taxi. This had been all about trust? Sure it had.

Not once did she protest or call me names, she just cuddled up and shivered in my arms.

Moghul came and discussed it all and I managed to stay sane and calm and nod and say some logical things. I pulled it off and convinced him we were good to go.

Subdrop was the last bit of wisdom he gave me. I filed it away.

When we reached the marina, Jodie had to walk a bit for us to get to the boat, stumbling with my arm around her, and when we found the boat, I almost unraveled there and then.

I fucked up. Yeah, I did, but I had to get her home and safe. I couldn't fall apart yet. I was going to, I knew it. But first, get her home. I'd not felt this stupid and fragile for many years. Not since I was a teenager and a gang had beaten me to a pulp in a back yard one day. I'd picked myself up after that. This time…this time I was sunk so deep in a black chasm, I didn't know if there was a way out.

How could I have done that? How? So wrapped in the scene when she was terrified. Not scared. Not in that halfway balance between pain and pleasure. Terror had been in her eyes. In the whole of the last month, I'd never seen her look that scared.

I wrenched my fingers into my hair hard enough to pull on my face skin and stared down at her where she lay huddled under a blanket on the boat's padded seat. I'd failed her. I couldn't decide when caring for her had become so important, but it had. I clamped down on the anguish, wiped my nose and turned to start the engine.

But inside me was a bubbling mess. Sad, horrified at myself. Then mix in more sadness. Did I love her? Seemed unlikely, especially since I wasn't sure what love was really. But maybe I did. And if I did…love her, that made it worse.

My plan was clear. Home. Get her settled. Then fuck off forever.

Of course it wasn't that simple. We got back to the island and I drove her home, even got her into bed, after a warm shower, with the sheets tucked under her chin. I looked down and thought absurdly how all she needed was a teddy bear to complete the picture. Then, all set to go, I looked up subdrop since Moghul had told me to before I left her.

Ah. Complicated. Subdrop was complicated. I stared at the screen.

"…the emotional and physical after-effects from the release and drop in the endorphins of the body after a BDSM play session."

Made sense though, after all she'd gone through tonight. It could lead to depression, anxiety and feelings of rejection in someone who played hard just once. How would it be after we played at TPE for a month, if I then walked out immediately after bringing her home?

I couldn't leave her alone. If anyone would get it she would, but I couldn't stay for long either. Why? Because I didn't trust myself anymore. I was not normal. I was not normal even by kinky standards. This month had shown me two things – that I was a sadist who liked hurting people, and that I couldn't control it when I let it loose.

I didn't even know if I was going to get all these dark desires back into the box they came from. This was like picking up the pieces after a suicide bomber has exploded. Nothing was ever going to be the same again.

Midnight ticked over on the bedside clock. We were back in the real world. The experiment was over.

I made myself sit with her in the bed. Moonlight let me see a little of her face on the pillow. Peaceful at last.

"Klaus." At sound of her voice something hurt inside me. She spoke so quietly. Was she afraid I wasn't here? "Can you hold me? Please?"

God. I could almost hear the crack as my heart fractured. I'd barely let her speak for a month. Now, of all times, she called to me like that. Like we were together. Like she trusted me still.

I wiped my eyes with my forearm. If my eyes didn't stop watering, I'd have to see a fucking eye specialist. I sighed. Then I slid down under the sheets and wrapped myself around her, breathing in her essence that one last time. She smelled so good. With my eyes closed, and my face buried in her hair, I tried to remember her scent, tried to catalogue it so I could recall it when I needed to. Then I did the same for the feel of her in my arms and the sound of her breathing. Soppy but true.

When I woke at the crack of dawn, I did what I'd decided to the night before. I organized her hard drive, and hid all the camera footage away under a password. I tidied up the house and packed my stuff in my suitcase that had gotten dusty in a spare room. I fed Baxter one last time. I found all the kinky shit and packed it up to take away with me, made sure she had food for few days, then I wrote out a long note for her that included the password, and I left it beside the bed.

Last move – I picked up the cat from where he was purring and doing figure of eights around my feet, and put him in bed with her. I frowned as he nudged his way under the covers. Maybe she didn't like cat hair on the sheets but, tough luck, that was my last act as her Master.

Then I left, taking everything with me that she no longer needed, including me.

* * * *

How do you start being someone who you used to be? Buggered if I knew. I had to start work again, didn't I? Walking out, not going back, did occur to me.

But the prospect of somehow starting my life over again was too crazy.

The prospect of abandoning life was even crazier. Not my style. Even if I seemed to have ended up at the bottom of a black hole.

And even if I seemed to have damaged the one person who now meant everything to me.

I think she always had meant more than I'd admitted to myself. I still wouldn't call it love. Love was for the weirdos of the world who wanted to label things. Whatever it was we had, I didn't want to leave her unprotected. What we'd done would affect her badly. If it left me stranded in a dark wasteland with my heart bleeding on the ground, what would it do to her?

I'd systematically stripped her of her defenses. Running away was not an option for me. I'd stay and do what I could without stepping in and being a crutch for her. She had to stand up again on her own.

So. My locum was leaving this morning. I'd arranged to have him come in to get paid today. I'd open up the business, do what I did to earn a living, arrange a few things, get on with life. Forget I was a sadistic bastard. Pray I was whole enough to function.

ᴄ Chapter Twenty-one ᴄ

Jodie

A warm lump vibrated against my back. Baxter. I smiled. That cat was getting more and more demanding. The light filtering through my closed eyelids and the coolness said morning sometime. I shifted beneath the sheet. Aches and sharp twinges all over my body stirred.

Ow. Last night. I remembered, running through what had happened, bliss, BDSM, me being deliciously dominated, and then my memory blurred. Something had happened when Kat went to stick a needle in me. I'd been scared but Klaus had stopped her. Klaus…

I sat up and looked around. Where was he? The rest of the bed was cold. The house was silent of the sounds of another person living in it. It felt empty. Had he gone somewhere?

I was utterly awake and aware in a heart-seizing fraction of time. The room around me sprang into bright relief.

Where was he?

In a few sweeping seconds, I spotted the pile of stuff on the bedside table and some paper with writing on it scrawled in his hand. The date at the top – the day my fantasy ended. I grabbed the paper and let the sheet float onto the bed. The first words were galling.

I can't be with you without hurting you. I'm not safe. Don't follow me. I won't leave you instructions as that would defeat the purpose. Remember who you are. How you used to live.

I stared. The next words were crossed out.

Forget what we did.

The rest was nothing important or nothing that seemed so – it was all about passwords and the film and something called subdrop and what I could do.

Doing anything seemed wrong.

I let out a shuddery breath and clutched the sheet to my chest. I was alone. It wasn't just the house that was empty, it was me.

Cold seeped into my bones, froze my muscles, pained me so badly my stomach grew claws. I hurt. I hurt so much.

I got underneath the sheet and buried my eyes in the darkness.

∽ *Chapter Twenty-two* ∾

Klaus

Monday went by. I paid my locum. I worked. I stared out my window, a lot. I wondered what she was doing. I couldn't be with her. I was dangerous around her, but depression could hit some people hard. For once the palm trees lining the beach road didn't make me smile. She needed someone to talk to. I knew some of her friends. I texted them. Arranged things. Told a heap of white lies.

Lunchtime. I was eating a chicken sandwich at my desk and wondering why it was making me feel ill. Lifting the top layer revealed chicken and butter. Dead flesh. *Ugh.*

What might she do, by herself? I made my jaw work, chewing over and over, and I swallowed. It went down in a lump. I was a vulture. Maybe I should have a label on my head that said, *Carnivore. Beware of the teeth. It bites.*

The remains of the sandwich placed to one side, I rested my forehead on the heels of my hands.

Would she try to see me?

I thought about hiring a security guard. I think that was what's called a what-the-fuck moment. I caught myself in time. What was I scared of? Jodie? Myself? A security guard wouldn't help me against either of those.

Chapter Twenty-three

Jodie

For the third time that day, the knocking then banging on the front door awoke me. There was nobody but me to answer it. I sighed and dragged myself from bed.

Clothes, needed some. Naked, I rummaged through my cupboard and drawers. The denim shorts went on only to be pulled off when I spied the bruises on my legs. Jeans. Had to be jeans. A T-shirt would do, though.

I combed my hair with my fingers and found my way to my front door.

Adrianna was on the other side. Bright white-and-blue strappy dress and her expression seemed to bubble over with enthusiasm.

"Hi! Jodie where have you been? It's been a whole month! You said you'd be away, but a month with no phone, email, nothing?" She hugged me then brushed past in mini-tornado mode. "Klaus texted me this morning. Said you'd broken up, again. When will you two learn? Isn't this the second time in a few years? He said you needed someone to lean on."

As she talked she marched toward the kitchen pulling me in her wake like a giant spaceship with one of those tractor beams glued to my ass. "But, hey girl, least he cares. My exes just vanished over the fucking horizon!"

Bemused and tired, I followed.

"You got coffee? I neeed coffee. I'll make and you..." She yanked open the fridge door. "Can pile the Tim Tams on a plate. You can do that can't you?" She eyed me. I must have looked bedraggled. "Hmm. Maybe not. Still chocolate biscuits fix everything!"

Now that was probably going to be engraved on Adrianna's gravestone. Though blonde, tattooed, and skinny as any surfer chick, she ate chocolate by the truckload.

Jug boiled, coffee made, biscuits piled, we sat down at the dining room table.

"Tell me all." Her instant sad face resonated within me. "Tell Auntie Adrianna and I'll make it all better."

We'd stopped moving, stopped talking. The activity had made the immensity of my feelings go away for a while.

I was alone in my house. How could that be? The table, the floor near the chair he used to sit in, even the sound of the surf outside reminded me of our month together when he'd made me his slave. Not fantasy slave. Not pretend. Real. Now he'd gone. Was it me?

I searched through memories. Was it the party? I remembered very little toward the end but I had a feeling something jarring had happened. What, though? I must have done something wrong and yet somehow Klaus thought it was his fault. The weight of all this seemed to drag at my body, at my face. All I wanted to do was to crumple to the floor and cry. Maybe I could go beg him to take me back. But the note had been so final.

How could he do that? Cutting us apart so easily, like it had been nothing. I wanted it back. I wanted to be his again.

Was I mad?

Yes, probably.

"Jodie?" She gently touched my hand where I rested it on my coffee mug. "That bad? Things get better, ya know? It won't last. Never does. You'll get over him."

I eyed her. She didn't know a thing. I couldn't tell her anything that wasn't a lie. So I smiled a lifeless smile, the best I could summon. "Thanks. I know. Thank you for coming."

I was thankful. People who were friends like this counted. But not enough. So I tried not to show how alien she seemed to me, and we chatted about nothing for a while. Then I shooed her away with promises that we'd get together and do something soon – dance club, girls night out, invasion of Cuba, whatever.

I went back to bed, but at least this time I read all of his note. I didn't cry, I was too disconnected to cry. None of this was real.

But I put the sim card back in my cellphone like he suggested. I checked out what subdrop was on the net. Huh. Yeah, I sure had all those symptoms.

I was cold, lonely, dead inside, but I didn't need any of the suggested treatments. All I needed was him. So I speed dialed his number and got nothing. No answer. Texting was the same.

Baxter meowed at me and I shot him a sour look. Had I been left this menace purely to get me to live? I wouldn't have been surprised. But I trudged into the kitchen, opened a sachet of food and poured it out. The cat food reminded me of eating. Baxter liked the stuff. I sniffed it.

As some sort of weird revenge against Klaus for abandoning me, I put a spoonful in my mouth. Uck.

I spit it out in the sink then leaned over with the water running, rinsing my mouth and spitting for the next minute.

"Fuck you, Klaus," I muttered, arms propped either side of the sink. "Fuck you to hell and back."

Damn. If he was here, I would've been caned for that.

I wished so much he was here.

The first tear rolled down my cheek. Stiffly, angrily, I wiped it away but another followed like some stupid product rolling off an assembly line.

"Go away," I growled at my tears. "Go away!"

They kept coming, filling my eyes, dripping into the sink, wetting my chin, my shirt.

At last the sorrow broke through and I sobbed out loud. I stayed there for ages, crying into the sink, then I gave in and folded up, sliding my back down the cupboard and sitting on the floor with my head hanging in my hands. The tears filtered through my fingers like rain.

"Why didn't you at least *talk*? Why?" The words echoed in my head.

They were plastic words that meant nothing, but I kept saying them when the tears choked me up so much that I stopped crying. Then I gripped my jeans hard until I hurt the flesh underneath. No one heard me crying and asking inane questions except the cat, who lay next to me in a curled-up bundle, purring his little heart out.

When I finally ran out of tears, I sat staring at the floor until the daylight went.

I heaved myself to my feet. Dark outside, mosquitoes were whining, my body was one huge, hot, prickly balloon. It seemed too big, as if my fingers were too far away and not mine. I shivered. Tired, so tired. I should eat.

I washed my face, stuck my head under the tap, and wiped my wet hair with a towel. Then I went back to bed. Being hungry seemed a good punishment.

I drifted off.

∽ *Chapter Twenty-four* ∾

Klaus

Tuesday, one of her friends, Adrianna, phoned to say Jodie was shaky but good. Shaky? I fended off her questions and hung up when I could. They could think what they liked. If I said too much it might contradict whatever story Jodie made up.

The "shaky" description had me googling again though. Never, never trust your first google. Subdrop could last for days. I'd known friends with long-term depression. How could I tell if this was worse than a fleeting problem? I doodled holes in the notepad on my desk for a while. I couldn't, could I? Not the way I'd severed all ties.

Half wondering if I was justifying something I longed to do anyway, I answered one of her emails.

If you need me for anything, Jodie. You can text me or email. Just nothing physical, though. No meeting. No chats online. Would you like to do that?

I waited nervously for her reply, checking my inbox every fifteen minutes until I saw her answer.

Yes. Thank you.

Those simple words sank into me like a stone settling to the bottom of a pool. My mind went quiet. I could have kissed the laptop screen.

I wasn't sure what I'd been afraid of…that she'd suicide? Maybe. Guess I had. Guess I needed this contact as much as she did. Without it I'd be wondering what she was up to.

Her next email was simple, and one word: *Why?*

It took me an hour of typing and deleting a long and complex answer several times, before I gave in and mailed off my reply.

I'm afraid I will hurt you. I did hurt you at the play party.

Her answer arrived later that night.

Not really. No more than I liked. The party was amazing. If I did something wrong, please *please* tell me.

I read it over and over. She was still confused about my reasons. It seemed as if she'd forgotten what Kat had almost done to her. The terror on her face had been real. I knew it had. Should I bring it up if she'd forgotten? What justification did I have for such cruelty? None.

So I answered in general terms again. I told her, I stressed, that she'd done nothing wrong.

That she was sad and lost was clear – as clear as it was that I was the same. This was such a farce. A comedy of ridiculousness. Her next answer jolted me.

Jodie: *Please come back.*

Fuck. A fork in the eye had nothing on this. I needed a heart surgeon to come do some quick cutting. Right then, mine hurt so much, I'd rather have it out.

Me: *No. You have to learn to stand on your own feet again.*

What I was feeling – how thick I'd been thinking she was the only dependent one. This wasn't one-sided. I wanted to be with her.

Then I tried to find out if she was eating and taking care of herself without being too specific.

Her answers were as non-specific as my questions. When, in frustration, I asked her exactly what she'd eaten and done that day, Jodie gave me a list of everything in great detail. And she left it hanging, as if to say, do you approve?

I sat back in my chair.

I'd forgotten how smart she was.

Here I was, trying to keep distant when she was cunningly doing the opposite. I didn't answer. After an hour, she did. At two AM Wednesday morning.

Jodie: *Please, Klaus. I know how much you liked what we were doing. I want to serve you naked again. I want your hand in my hair and I want want WANT you to do whatever you wish to my body.*

Yeah, I'd sure managed to pull away from her. That alone had given me a hard-on.

Wednesday was a day of tiredness.

I made myself be distant yet helpful. I stuck to my guns and stayed in the zone I imagined halfway between not being there for her at all, and being in her face, kissing her, fucking her, feeling her body. *Damn.*

Thursday, she was making little sarcastic jokes. Her true personality returned. As soon as I was certain, over the next emails that day, I told her I was doing it, going to truly *go*. Her replies became terser, angrier. Anger was good. I let it ride, even when she called me the misbegotten offspring of a hunch-backed koala and a camel. *Ah.* Definitely, the return of the sense of humor. I said goodbye. After my last email, I swallowed despite the dryness of my throat. She needed more than what I could give her.

Though it pained me to reach out to him, I emailed Moghul and asked if he could somehow, quietly, get someone to talk to Jodie. She wasn't on Fetlife so I had to give her email to him. But, I knew her so well. Kink wasn't a minor flutter for her. She needed some sort of insight and some help to see where she was going. Maybe, she needed another Dom?

That idea made me want to hurt someone again. Not her though, the imaginary *him*.

By the Friday afternoon, I was mostly numb, yet scared. I had to teach at the club.

Being an automaton at work was far easier than at the club. There, it was all numbers, clients with money concerns, and Marjorie, a secretary who was as old as the hills and more into knitting and cooking than sex. I wasn't about to molest anyone.

Here though, there were people who loved life. People who knew me as the fun guy who taught them how to flatten each other in a good, repeatable, professional way. Judo was tripping with finesse. Or so I told them when we were being all casual at the club BBQs.

I pushed open the glass door and braced myself as Ted came storming down the hallway with a grin on his face.

"Good holiday?"

"Sure was." I smacked his shoulder. "How's the class?"

"Waiting for you, sensei. There's one fresh face. Gavin. He's from Mackay."

"Okay."

I made small talk as we walked.

What if I had this urge to hurt people here? Women specifically. My heartbeat was scaling the walls in urgency. Clearing the mind of evil thoughts was necessary before entering the dojo, but I doubted myself so badly. By the time I stood at the front of the class, with my black obi wrapped correctly and my white judogi neat, I was calm. The smell of the dojo thrilled me. So long, it had been. I was back.

"Sensei ni. Rei!"

They bowed. A now silent rank of kneeling judoka waited for me.

Slowly, I surveyed them, smiling grimly. Young, old, women, men. Nothing.

Nothing. Normal.

If I was a giggler, I would have burst out there and then. I had no absurd need to hurt people. I could control it this far at least. Around Jodie was another matter.

And if I explored further by entering the BDSM community? I had no doubt it would be the same with anyone else who was stupid enough to let me practice on them. The pull of it was extreme. Just remembering what we'd done, some of the scenes, the way she'd looked when she climaxed and when she let me command her... When I had hurt her.

No. I was done.

One week down, and now I had the rest of my life to live. If only it hadn't become so monotone. For a month, with Jodie, I'd discovered color. Zingy, meat-raw, blown-sky-high *color*. Life after that was black and white and as tasteless as the chicken sandwich.

∾ Chapter Twenty-five ∾

Jodie

Thursday night, I'd hauled myself out of the depression and done some organizing. Klaus was done with me? Good...fine, wonderful, *good*.

Okay, it wasn't good, but I'd gotten busy busy busy, figuring that scampering around would keep me from dwelling on it all too much. I am woman hear me roar, and all that. I'd been tempted to delete all the files with camera footage but hadn't, yet. We'd been far too extreme for me to be able to easily turn it into a doco, or so I told myself. Was I avoiding looking at it? Probably.

Would I ever look at it?

I stared at the monitor and the files in my pictures folder. Probably not. Still, I could face this now. Life. I'd regrown my spine, hadn't I? With a couple of mouse clicks, I shut down the PC.

My calendar was now thriving with engagements. A few appointments to see if I could get into a regular job doing documentaries, a place in a comedy tour going into the outback towns and down into New South Wales. Maybe even a place touring overseas if my luck held. If.

Let's face it, I was still going to be eating beans soon. The outback tour was a crap one that'd earn me a pittance for basically getting heckled every second night. I'd wasted a month, let myself have the most demeaning, most painful things done to me, and all for footage I couldn't use. And Klaus had walked out on me.

Without explaining why. That was what hurt the most. That he hadn't even bothered to *say*. I'd asked him and only received answers that perplexed me more.

I stared at the PC screen again, like it could sit up and answer all my deep and meaningful questions. I shut my eyes. Like it could tell me why I craved what he'd done. It bothered me. When I wondered about him, the same question popped up. Did he blame me? Had I done something wrong, something bad? Or, and this one seemed more and more possible the more I thought about it, did he blame himself in some way? The note had pretty much stated that.

I can't be with you without hurting you. I'm not safe.

I couldn't understand truly *why* because he hadn't explained. Now he'd blocked my calls, and didn't answer texts or emails. My next step would be to turn up at his apartment, but even to me that seemed too desperate. Because facing him turning me away from his home would likely devastate me.

I wasn't a stalker, was I?

I sniffed back tears. They hadn't come much the last few days, just sometimes when I was lonely. Maybe Adrianna was right and I should go out with the girls?

Or maybe, I should answer the emails that had been sitting in my inbox for days. I could even see one from Moghul and one from, of all people, Kat, or FieryKat as she called herself on Fetlife. I knew about Fetlife though I hadn't joined. It seemed full of scary people, Kat included. How had they gotten my email? One possibility emerged – Klaus.

Was this him trying to help me?

I leaned back in the chair and folded my arms, did some rocking back and forth, maybe hoping that would jar my obviously decrepit brain into working. In a week and a half this tour started. In a week I could knuckle down and see if there was anything in the footage I could use. There must be friggin days of footage, even if he had turned off the cameras after he got really kinky. If I drummed up the courage, and edited severely, I could have a bestseller in there.

'Kay. I stuck my knuckle in my mouth and bit down, stayed that way until the pain got to me. Then I reached out and turned the computer back on. *Go, Jodie. Let's become a BDSM porn star. Not.*

The first file was the first day. Those bits were boring. So, heart thumping away, sweat at my temples, I jumped ahead and looked at a later file.

Through my fingers caging my eyes, I watched myself, naked, getting cropped by Klaus while my hands were tied overhead. Ohmigod, I melted into the chair and slouched there, riveted. Then I switched and watched him – he was so enthralled in what he did that he never looked away from me once.

When the video file ended, I rested my chin on my hands, thought awhile then announced my decision out loud, in a very firm voice, as if that made it a fairytale wish that would magically come true.

"I have to go see him."

What we had might have been perverted by the average person's standards, but I wanted it back. I wanted to see if we could be together, somehow. Not just me and any random Dom, I wanted to be together with Klaus. But I could see the problem now there was distance. Our month together had been artificial and, in the end, that had hurt us both, maybe even, I had a sudden thought, maybe Klaus more than me?

He was a formidable man, so what had made him run like that? I'd ask him to his face.

After all, what could he do if I accosted him at his home? Uh. Yeah. Lots of nasty things, possibly. Somewhere else then? If I was determined, I could do this.

* * * *

The office was the best in-between place where I could find Klaus. Not too personal. Not too private.

So, here I was, on the beach across the road from the office, in a Mexican sombrero and big sunglasses plus an itsy bitsy mauve bikini top and purple skintight shorts. The office closed at midday on Saturdays, so just before that, I sauntered across the road.

Only, to my dismay, the plaque with the opening hours said it closed at eleven thirty. *Shit.*

I knocked on the glass door but the secretary was gone and no one answered. Frantic, I walked around to the side window and peered in. *Oh, thank God.*

He was in there still. I unfolded and plastered my sign against the window, then I tapped. I took off the sombrero and the sunglasses. He was just getting up from his chair when he saw me. His gaze locked on mine.

I desperately wanted to emphasize the importance of this, my need, but couldn't think of a way, so I merely swiveled the paper on the glass a little, and I waited, trying not to shake, trying to look lost and forlorn.

Which I was.

The sign was simple: *Meet me at the park. Please. I HAVE to talk. I beg you.*

I stared some more then he nodded. The hairs on the back of my neck rose. Cold shivers ran all the way down my arms. He'd said yes. *Oh fuck.*

The park was up the hill a little to the right, farther along the beach road. We'd often met there to share a picnic lunch back in the days when we were couple.

Even next to the beach, with the breeze coming off the water, it was hot at midday on Magnetic Island – especially hiking up a small hill. His jeep growled past me on the way and he never slowed at all. Okay, I could take that. He hadn't wanted to meet me. This was my idea.

It did hurt, though. This was what I could look forward to – more distancing, and more rejection. If he blamed himself and thought he was dangerous, I had to be ready to rebut his arguments. Think of this as a kinky debate. One that had our future riding on it.

The last twenty yards as I approached the bench where he sat were fraught with both a severe case of oh-my-god-what-am-I-going-to-say, and a joy that I'd see him again. The tree overhead left the seat in the coolness of shade and the ground covered in leaves that crunched underfoot.

I arrived to the sound of fractured leaves and the whine of the wind.

He'd draped himself with his arm along the back of the iron and slatted timber bench, with a big, long section un-sat in and unoccupied. I eyed it but wasn't game to sit. Though I wanted to so very much. The warm swell that built inside me as I waited before Klaus shook me. He was pretending I hadn't arrived, and watching something, or nothing, in the distance.

The wind flung my hair across my face, and I pulled it from my mouth, then I waited until the tension tore at my heart too much. "Sir?"

His eyes were sadder but still pretty, if a man's could be called that. The long pants and button-up cotton shirt from work emphasized his masculinity. There were muscles under there, ones that could hold me down with ease while he did things to me, evil, nasty, wonderful things. I wanted to touch his jaw and feel the stubble against my skin. I wanted to look up and see him looking down at me, his property.

"I'm not your Sir," he said gently. "What do you want, Jodie?"

Not. The negative made my eyes ache.

You, of course. I want you. I dredged up a better answer. "I want to know why you left me."

A pause. He seemed into letting me wait forever for his answers. I wasn't going away without them, even if he took a hundred years.

"I told you why."

"That didn't make sense." More silence. "Yes, you hurt me, but I wanted you to."

A frown slowly crept onto his brow. "You've forgotten that Kat wanted to stick a needle through your nipple? Maybe you have but that doesn't change anything. You were terrified. I knew it. I saw it and ignored it. I can't trust myself with you." Now he saw me properly, dissected me from my feet to my face. "Let me loose and one day I'd probably hurt you badly. I'm a sadist and a sociopath. Now do you understand?"

Uh. I remembered. I saw that needle again, at my breast. "Yes, she was scaring me, but you stopped her."

"Because she kept at me until I woke up. Are you wearing only that?"

"What?" Confused, I glanced down at my scanty clothes. "I've got a T-shirt." Maybe if I stuck out my chest and flirted?

"You'll get sunburnt. Put it on."

His concern for my well-being startled me and the sting returned to my eyes. He did still care. For a moment I let myself imagine he was still my Master and this was his command, but the feeling dwindled to a pitiful nothing. He wasn't, of course. It wasn't. This was nothing more than what he'd say to anyone. Despite the sombrero, my shoulders did feel burnt just from the walk here.

I sighed. Miserable, I took off the sombrero, found the T shirt in my cloth bag and pulled it on.

I understood now. More than I had.

He was so terribly patient with me. I might have had to drag him to this meeting but he was explaining this to me without yelling or looking angry. Even now he simply waited for me to process what he'd said. Like if maybe he got this told to me right and done with, he'd not have to repeat it? He was wrong though, wasn't he?

Eyes half-shut, still puzzling over the ramifications, I shook my head. "I remember that – Kat, the needle, and being really panicky, but you stopped her, you stopped yourself." I looked in his eyes. "You never truly hurt me more than I could stand. It was part of what made it all worthwhile for me. I liked it." I searched for a word, clenched my fist to my chest. "I reveled in it. I want it to be *us* again. Please. Please, try."

"No. I want you to contact Moghul or Kat though. I gave them your email. Talk to them. I think perhaps you do need someone. Just not me. It's over, Jodie." He raised his hand toward me, as if he'd been struck by the urge to touch.

"Over? No. No, please." If I could communicate the depth of my need with my eyes I would have. I should show him with some other gesture. I slipped to my knees in the grass and dirt. "Sir. Please. Let us try again."

"No," he grated out, and for once I could see the depth of the pain on his face.

Oh God. It hurt me to see that and *know*. He was hurting, more than me.

How selfish had I been? I'd organized this month-long experiment without a thought as to how it might affect him. He seemed so strong, yet I'd seen torture in his expression. If he'd let me I would have gone to him and hugged him, kissed him, drawn his arms around me so we were together again in the way a man and woman should be. Whole.

Something twisted inside me. Awareness blossomed.

That was the moment my heart truly let him in. I saw him as a man, not just my Master, because he needed me. I wanted more than just to kneel for him. I wanted to help him when he was sad, to be there for him, to make the pain go away.

I raised my head. "Please." This time, my heart and my soul bled out into my eyes.

But he stood and stepped back like I had some disease that might infect him. "Go home, Jodie."

And he walked away.

Dismayed, I watched him go.

What could I do? Nothing. It had been useless. I'd achieved nothing much at all except for understanding. I understood how hopeless this was. How implacable his stance. I'd not convince him in a century of begging.

Every part of my body seemed disassociated from the real me.

Oh, and I'd achieved one other paltry thing. I'd found out I loved him.

I picked myself up, dusted off my knees, sat in a crumpled heap on the bench, and thought a long time. Only one or two tears slipped down my face. Then I went home. I had no idea what I should do. None, at all.

☙ Chapter Twenty-six ❧

Klaus

Funny how they called it nursing a beer, but it fitted. The thing had gone flat long ago and I only hung onto it for something to do. The outdoor beer garden of the Yellow Cockatoo Hotel was crowded enough that I could sit by myself and not be noticed in all the noisiness. The night air was crisp and filled with the scent of tropical flowers hanging off the trellises, barbecued meat from the kitchens, the sound of mingled voices, and now and then the distant roll of waves on the shore. I was peaceful yet alone, yet also empty.

Give it another year maybe, I'd be over it.

Jodie was here somewhere. I'd seen her inside with some of her girlfriends, including the craziest one, Adrianna. Though on a crazy scale the other two were up there in the nine out of ten range too. The island's smallness meant seeing each other was unavoidable. So I hadn't bothered doing anything more than move out here under the stars where the lights were dimmer.

"Hello, Klaus."

Shit. I almost jumped. I eyed Jodie. She was breathtaking, as always. The short blue dress suited her – showing off her long legs and gorgeous feminine muscles. Again, there came that tightness as I imagined what I could do to her…if I had her.

I swallowed some beer, checked her out again, decided to meet her head on. We were adults. We could figure this out. Even if having my guts pulled out inch by inch would hurt me less. Just holding her for a moment would heal my world. *Do. Not. Touch.*

"Hello, Jodie. Not Sir anymore?"

Such a bold look in her eyes. "Not until you say so…Klaus."

She flicked back her hair from her shoulders then slid into the chair opposite me. Her curls bounced in glossy waves. I remembered the cool feel of her hair sliding through my fingers.

There was no glass in her hands, her voice was unslurred, her movements were simply those of a young, beautiful woman. "Not drinking tonight?"

I guess I'd half-expected her to fall back into her old ways where she almost seemed to deliberately attempt to gain my sympathy by getting drunk.

"No. I'm being good."

"Oh? Glad to hear that."

"Yes. I can help you better when I'm sober." She'd said that so matter-of-factly that it took me a second to digest it.

What the hell?

I put my glass down on the coaster. "Can you now?" I suppressed a smile.

While I watched curiously, she took out her phone, dialed it and held it to her ear a moment. "Here." She held it out to me. "It's for you."

"Who? What are you trying to do?"

"It's Moghul. You convinced me I couldn't change your mind, so here. You need to talk to another man who can tell you the truth about yourself." She jiggled the phone at me. "Afraid, Mr. Big Bad Dom?"

"This is not a game," I growled.

"I know that." Carefully she placed the phone on the table beside my drink. "I do. This is important to me. I…care for you, a lot, and I am *not* giving up without a fight. Talk to him or I promise you, I will never leave you alone." Then she sat back in the chair, folded her arms beneath her breasts and glared at me.

I lifted one eyebrow. If looks could kill she'd just had a SWAT team take out her ass with extreme prejudice.

I picked it up, and squashed it to my ear so I could hear above the noise. "Hi."

"Hi yourself. Where are you?"

"Hotel. Jodie just gave me her phone and said to talk."

"Yeah, well, go find somewhere quieter. I'll wait. You do need to know some things."

I moved outside and sat on a brick fence. Jodie had followed and sat a few yards away but I ignored her for the moment. This was so intrusive, and yet I sensed the importance she placed on this. And I did value Moghul's opinion.

It wouldn't change me but maybe I could help set things up for her.

"Go ahead."

For a few seconds he said nothing. "Okay, I'll start with this. You and Jodie have been so foolish. Playing with fire is the best way I can put it. She told me about her documentary."

I grunted and listened some more.

"Yes, you could have hurt her badly, but mostly due to ignorance. What you did...BDSM is consensual, always. Playing around with that concept when you are new to it all. Terrible. Just terrible. I'm not surprised you've damaged yourself. But I can tell you this. You're not a sociopath. You're not a bad person. You're simply untrained and uninformed."

I put my fingers to the bridge of my nose, pressed down. "I wanted to see her bleed. She'd not given me permission and, man, I don't know if I'd have stopped if I were in the wrong situation, alone. I can't trust myself."

Quiet came for a moment.

"Some of us get closer to the dark edge than others. I promise you that with help, you'll discover how to be her Dom without overstepping the mark. I promise you. You just need boundaries and rules. If you're who I think you are, you can control yourself. If you're worried, keep it public until you're sure. There are ways, man, there *are*."

I took a long breath, exhaled. Damn. He made it sound doable. Not easy, but doable.

"After the party, I warned you about subdrop. Remember?"

"Yes, I do." I glanced at Jodie, waiting patiently, waiting like a good girl. My appreciation of her as a woman stirred to life again.

"I forgot to say that sometimes Doms, Tops, can get Top Drop."

"What the fuck? You're joking. That sounds like a wine."

I listened to him chuckle. "No, it's like subdrop though. I think you got it. Along with all the mistakes you let yourselves make, I'm not surprised. If I'd known what a mess you two were in, I'd never have let you in to play. Now, I want you and Jodie to talk about this. As far as I can tell, she wants you back, as her Dom."

"That's not news. Talking to her…" My head was stuffed full of all this new information. Did I believe him? No one knew me like I did. He hadn't been there. Still, a big *what-if* sign had lit up in my head. "Not sure that's a good idea."

"Klaus, I can't tell you what you have to do. Yes, people can get hurt physically because others have not thought things through, or have not done their homework, or because they are out-and-out sadists. We don't condone that in the community. If I thought that was you, I'd not be sitting out here on my patio getting eaten by mozzies when I could be watching the football. Think hard before you run away. If you were bad, you'd not have crashed like this. Caring is the crucial point. You care for her."

"Uh." Such an eloquent reply. I rummaged about and found some words. "Thanks. I'll see. Sorry for all the trouble."

He sighed. "Klaus. Fuck not ordering you. Go talk. Stop being an asshole."

He hung up.

Well, he got the asshole part right.

"Here." I held out the phone to her and she stepped over and took it, dropped it into her handbag.

Talk to her?

As likely as the sun exploding. I had a severe case of info overload. I wanted him to be right, but…but, but, but.

We looked at each other without speaking for a while.

If I said anything I'd give her false hope, but she'd been trying to help. Did I want to hurt her now by saying a flat no, or maybe later by stringing her along?

Jodie did that nervous thing where she played with a corner of her dress. I could see she was bursting to ask me.

I got in first. "Don't. Don't ask. You can't expect an answer. Just leave me be, to think." I found my car keys, pulled them out and jingled them. "Go back inside to your friends."

"Oh. Oh." Though she stared at me for ages, her shoulders slowly caved in. "I thought he might…I'm sorry." She shook her head. "If you change your mind, text me. Just say meet me, and I'll be here." For a second her gaze fixed hopefully on mine, then she turned away.

Misery was written in her every move. I worked my jaw and resisted grabbing her, enfolding her in my arms, and kissing away all that sadness.

Watching her walk away trampled severely on the remains of my resolve. I jabbed my thigh with the keys and hissed at the pain.

Leave now.

We were both a mess, but I couldn't see how to help her more without being with her. For a moment I was angry at Moghul. I'd wanted him to help her get her life back together, not to tell her how to get back with me. Unseeing, unfocused on anything except the confusion messing up my mind, I fumbled my way to my car, and started the engine.

* * * *

There are some things you have to take your time to digest, no matter what.

Believing takes time.

Jodie was doing well. I kept an eye on her via her friends. Adrianna seemed to think it was cute and I'm sure she told Jodie of my inquiries but it couldn't be helped. Besides, Jodie's plea had awakened me. I wasn't willing to say goodbye yet. The connection between us was stretched, and it was thin, but it was still there. I never forgot, on any day, that she was on the island somewhere, within reach.

Until the day she left on the tour.

She was gone. A small panic stewed inside me for three days until I gave in and called Moghul. I invited him to the island. What he'd said on the phone, with the music and laughter in the background, had seemed distant, trivial – like a saying you found in a fortune cookie, or one of those phone-a-friend last resort things you do on a game show. Yet what hinged on his words was so important. I wanted to hear it up close, where I could see his eyes.

We trudged across the cool morning sand at Horseshoe Bay with our surf skis and waded into the sea. The island was protected by the Great Barrier Reef so surf was non-existent. Getting out past the waves was a simple exercise most days. What waves? Surfers just shook their heads in dismay when they saw ours.

I took us out and around to Balding Bay at a good pace. We stopped a fair distance out from shore, paddles across our thighs, breathing hard, sweat beading on our skin.

"You ready to talk now, Klaus?" Moghul straightened and dipped his paddle in the sea on one side to curve the ski round to face me.

"Guess so."

For a man who said he rarely got the chance to take out a ski, Moghul still had the tight chest muscles of a man who exercised regularly. "You know, most days I have to stop myself calling you Santy Klaus."

I snorted. "Not Asshole Klaus?"

"That too. On occasion."

"Thank you for not rushing me."

"Wouldn't dream of it. Take your time. Only one thing." He tapped his fingers on the shaft of his paddle. "Just remember Jodie's a pretty woman. Some other Dom may snap her up if she decides to dip her toes back in the BDSM community."

Fuck no. "Huh. Over my dead body."

Moghul nodded soberly. "Think you've already made up your mind." He dabbed at the water again as a bigger wave rocked under our skis.

I grimaced, thinking some more. Farther out, a sea eagle speared into the water and rose up with a fish glinting in its talons. The rising sun beat flashes of light off the surface. The water was clear and blue, and a school of fish zipped past a long way down.

What if some other man did make a play for her?

"I doubt she could back away from kink now. Or even from TPE. We went at it hard and she was…" I rubbed my chin.

"Loving it?"

"Yeah."

We shared some more silence.

"Moghul, you're so patient you'd give a statue a run for its money."

"Nah. It's important. The mind's a funny thing. You haven't asked me again if you're a bad man or a sociopath."

"Ah." I sniffed and cleared my throat. After so many years as a pillar of the community, that was hard to get used to. "It's the sort of label I will never be sure of unless I try and fail." I eyed him. "I do not want to fail."

"Then don't. I told you how to play it safe."

"Public BDSM?" I turned the idea over. "I'm not sure it's for me. What we did with Kat and Damien was about my limit. You know? I'm not that much of an exhibitionist." I stroked into the water to turn my ski back toward Horseshoe Bay.

We put our backs into the strokes until the skis were sizzling through the water.

"You're overthinking it, Klaus."

I glanced across. "What do you mean?"

"Not everyone is into public or play parties. Kat would be more than happy to help you out. Think you could bear that?"

"Like an observer?" I thought while we powered along, getting into a nice matching rhythm. "I guess. Not Damien?"

"No! They split. He's found a Domme. So you'd trust her to teach you?"

"Teach? Hell, I wasn't thinking teaching. Just observing, you know? She can stop me if I go too far. I'd trust her to do that."

We rounded the point and caught sight of the farthermost spur of the super-long stretch of beach that was Horseshoe Bay.

Moghul laughed. "Sounds like a deal. But you better watch her too. She has designs on Jodie's ass."

"Yeah? I recall that." I grinned back at him. "That makes two of us then."

For the first time in ages, my heart lightened. Now I only had to tell her.

What if…what if I'd left it too long? She might say no. My little stew of panic came back and parked itself like a blob in my stomach. It would be pure, unadulterated karma if she did.

⌒ *Chapter Twenty-seven* ⌒

Jodie

My phone buzzed while I was gulping down some spring water in the little waiting room they'd given us. My act had gone down okay, thank God. I placed the bottle on the glass coffee table.

The screen showed Klaus was calling.

"Shit." I let my hand holding the phone flop to my lap. "It's him."

"Who?" asked Jane, the comedienne from Hobart, as she hopped on one leg adjusting the heel of her shoe.

"Old boyfriend."

"Oh?" She tottered back onto two feet. "Ahh. That's better. I'm up next. Oldies are goodies." She gave me a thumbs up. "Good luck with him. Break a leg!"

I rolled my eyes. "You too!"

I pressed answer, and put the phone to my ear, blanking out the distant cheers from the audience, then I strolled toward the door that led out to the parking lot. Despite my casual attitude, I was nervous as hell.

All I could hear was the audience. Even after the door swung shut, the other end was silent. I swallowed, checked the screen. Yes, it was Klaus.

"Hi." I settled my shoulders against the cold brick of the outside wall. It was quiet out here apart from distant cars on the highway. "Hey, Klaus, for this sort of call you're supposed to breathe heavier, you know?"

He chuckled.

And my heart ceased to beat, just for a second. I laid my palm over my chest as if to calm my heart. *Oh my God. That husky tone.* I'd heard him say so many things. I clamped down on the vivid memories…the dark, pain-edged, orgasmic ones. I shivered.

Stop, stop, stop, stop, stop. Be calm.

"How are your shows going?"

"Good."

"Glad to hear it."

Fuck. You didn't ring me just to ask that did you?

I massaged my forehead.

What else would he ask? Hope was banging at my head screaming just a bit.

"Hey, Klaus."

"Yes?"

Here goes. "Is this a…a good sign? You ringing me?"

Pause.

"Yes. I think so. I've talked to Moghul again. It depends on whether we're still on the same wavelength."

"Wavelength?" I giggled with relief, mad elation, and stupidity too, maybe. "Is this a physics lesson or a kinky-as-shit phone call about us, like, doing kinky things together again?"

Talk about laying it on the table. The phone shook; my hand shook, as I waited for his reply.

"Guessing here but, the second one. A kinky-as-shit phone call."

"Good," I whispered. I wiped away the tears meandering down my face. "Good." I sniffed.

"You crying, Jodie?"

"Yes."

"I'm sorry. I'm so sorry –"

"Don't be. Please don't be."

Pause. "Okay. But Jodie, you're back tomorrow, aren't you? Flying back?"

"Yes." Now my pulse was hammering so hard I could barely breathe.

"Then I'll meet you where you said last time. You said if I changed my mind you'd meet me there."

Suddenly I remembered – outside the hotel. "Oh! Sure. When?"

"Tomorrow night. Eight PM."

"What should I wear?"

"You're asking for instructions?"

That woke me up. "Umm. Um, yes?"

"Wear something pretty. A dress. No panties."

Then he hung up.

Hell. I stared at the phone, then I pressed it within both my hands and squeezed. "That sounds good."

Damn, I wanted a plane, fast. "Where's the batman spotlight in the sky when you need one?"

I was going to *die* before tomorrow.

∽ Chapter Twenty-eight ∽

Klaus

I made sure to arrive before she could. Eight PM in a poorly lit car park outside a hotel wasn't the place to leave a woman alone. When she emerged from the hotel entrance wearing the same blue dress as that other night, I smiled.

"Hi," she said quietly as she approached. The closer she came the more my guilt surfaced. She was thinner, if more confident than when she'd been my slave, but anxiety lurked in the straightness of her mouth and the way her eyes searched mine.

"Hi, yourself."

I stepped close, and with the smallest of pressure, tipped up her chin with my forefinger. The trembling beneath my finger said a lot. I gently tucked some loose strands of her hair behind her ear. Hugging would have helped her, perhaps, and me certainly, but I didn't have that right, not yet.

"We're going to go sit on the beach and talk. That is, if you're agreeable?" I twitched my eyebrows upward, and I prayed.

If she was here, she was most likely agreeable, but still, us humans are strange. Had she changed her mind? Maybe she'd come to say goodbye? Maybe she just wanted to kick my shins and stalk off fuming? Maybe I'd get shafted like I probably deserved.

She licked her lips and made a funny little noise in her throat. "I...uh yes, I'm agreeable. Of course I am. You know I wanted you back."

That little statement sent my heart thumping faster.

I stooped and kissed her on her mouth, a slow, gentle kiss. "Remember when we made up those rules all that time ago about your capture fantasy? I said no abduction because it'd be too dangerous?"

She nodded, her eyes dark.

"I'm fixing that now. Don't scream." Then I ducked and picked her up with her top half dangling over my back and her legs held down by my arm. She gasped once. For a second I braced my muscles – a woman isn't light, and besides I liked the soft weight and scent of her there, caught over my shoulder. I restrained myself from turning my head to bite the side of her ass.

"Good girl," I whispered. "Consider yourself abducted."

Then I crossed the road with my little captive and strode through the thin gathering of palm trees and down onto the beach where I set her on her feet.

"That was pretty amazing." Jodie giggled. "Am I in the harem of the Prince of Zanzibar now?"

"Is that my rival? The Prince of Zanzibar? I'll remember that name. No, we're still on Magnetic Island, but…" I took her hand "… we are about to begin a new adventure. And we need to talk about it, because this time we both get to make up the rules."

We left our shoes by the footpath and ventured onto the cool sand, sitting in the softer drier zone halfway between the trees and where the waves surged up and down on the beach. A few ghost crabs toddled about sideways.

"Can we just hold hands for a minute?" she asked. "I want to feel you touching me. It will mean a lot to me."

"Sure. I'd like that too."

Her smile caught the moonlight and lifted my heart. I heard her inhale deeply before she put out her hand.

Those delicate fingers resting in mine – I hadn't realized how much I'd missed them. We sat together, her thigh resting against mine and we looked out across the sea.

I could barely believe she was here.

Slowly, the never-ending soft roar of the waves coming in and going out smothered the thoughts in my head. I licked the salt off my lips. The important ideas stuck up above the rest of my thoughts like the dinghies moored out there, rocking on the water.

I squeezed her fingers. "First. This is new, and not what we had before. Negotiation is a crucial part of BDSM. And it has to be consensual. That's the absolute bedrock. You're a part of this. Where do you want to start?"

"Oh. Umm. Anywhere you like. I think maybe that's best."

I held back a laugh. "Not quite what I meant."

"Hmm. I guess I need time to think through this idea."

"Now that's a good decision already. There's only one thing I feel I should mention now in case it bothers you. There's going to be someone watching us whenever we do scenes. Until I can trust myself."

"Oh. That's going to be…curious. Umm, who?"

"Kat." I waited. If that was a problem, I'd have to think of someone else.

"Her?" she squeaked out. "She wanted to take my ass home."

"Yes. Her. But I won't let her take your ass home because it will be my ass."

Jodie snorted. "I guess that's okay then. Least she's already familiar with all our…bits."

"Exactly. Moghul trusts her. And she had some interesting ideas that night. Maybe you'd let her play too, sometimes?"

Jodie hesitated. "Maybe."

"Oh?" For a second I allowed that old sadistic me to rear his head and I thrilled at the thought of what Kat might want to do to Jodie. "So long as you never forget you belong to me."

"I won't…Sir." I could hear amusement in her voice.

"But now." I raised her hand and kissed her knuckles. "Tonight I want to just be with you."

"Yes. Mmm." Her sigh was beautiful. She pressed closer until her body leaned into mine and her head rested on my shoulder.

She was next to me again. Living, breathing, my Jodie.

I would find a way to make this work, even if I had to tunnel my way up from hell itself to make things right. I pulled gently until she lay down with her head in my lap.

After a while, she whispered up at me. "No panties, remember? Though..." She wriggled. "I don't want sand up my hoohah."

"No? I guess even us sadists don't do that. You tempt me, though. Wait until I have you ass up, naked, and bound." I froze as the image spun into my head and had to turn down my internal lust setting before I could go on. *One day. One day soon.* I shifted position. "We're going to do this slow. I'm not touching you until we go visit Moghul."

"Oh. Not at all?" I could almost hear the pout in her voice.

I chuckled then leaned in and brushed my lips on hers. I pressed small kisses on her until she opened her mouth. "Maybe just a little, like this."

She snuggled her fingers beneath mine again where they cradled her jaw. "I like that."

"Mm-hmm. I should think so. Now sit still so I can do it again. It's been so long." I thumbed the side of her soft mouth then traced the line of her eyebrow. "I want to make sure you remember that you're mine."

"Am I?" In the soft moonlight I could barely make out the fine wrinkling of her forehead. "Are you sure?"

She was taunting me. And that was so novel. So interesting. The beast in me sat up and growled. I'd given her very little leeway before but this had possibilities. "I think you're trying to provoke me."

"Mm-maybe. It's not as if you can *do* anything."

Glee bubbled up. I inched my fingers into her hair, twisted until she squealed then leaned in again until I could murmur in her ear. "You shouldn't tease a sadist. My 'maybe just a little' just got made bigger."

"Oops. And ouch! Let go!" But I could feel her shaking with suppressed laughter.

"Never."

Kissing her like a new lover was done with. I hesitated for a second, taking stock without undoing the twist of my fingers in her hair, making sure I wouldn't go too far. Then I released just a little of that other nastier *me*.

I took her mouth like I was a monster barely holding back from turning her over, yanking up her dress, and screwing her until she couldn't walk. When she was gasping and moaning and had bent up her knees so she could dig her toes in the sand, I drew away.

"That's my girl." I looked at the suggestion of cleavage and farther, down the length of her body. "It's dark enough here. I should pull down your dress and bite your nipples."

She went still.

It was all very well making threats, but I shouldn't. I knew, I shouldn't. I exhaled. "And, perhaps not. We'll wait."

"Oh." Her disappointment was obvious.

"I'm sorry, but it's for the best."

"So it's just to be kissing?"

I narrowed my eyes, staring down at her, playing lightly with her hair, and wondering at the change in her tone. She'd said that like a judge questioning a witness.

"Yes. For a while. Now shush and relax, and we can be here for a while."

"But then we go home, together?"

My grip tightened on her hair. I so wanted to turn her over and spank her. There it was though – my irrational need to hurt her for what? Being normal and having an opinion?

"No." I let out a measured breath. "I go to my apartment and you to your house."

"Oh."

I could almost hear her thinking, and I waited for her next question with some unease.

"Can we discuss this tomorrow, in daylight, at my house? I'll have Adrianna come over, so you can feel safe from me. She can sit out on the back verandah while we talk. She'll do it for me."

She'd said that so steadily, I wasn't sure if it was a tease or not.

"Safe? From you? You are pushing it."

"It's true though. You are scared of getting close, doing things. Well?"

"Damn." I glowered, though no doubt it was wasted in the darkness. "Okay. We do need to talk more. With Adrianna there, okay. Now be quiet and enjoy the bloody sea."

That time she giggled. I smiled despite my annoyance.

When we rose to go home and walked up the beach hand in hand, I was reluctant to let her go. But her hand slipped from mine and we said goodbye. I would see her tomorrow. More talking only, maybe I would kiss her again. It seemed like we'd reverted to being teenagers, or worse. Except the yearning inside me wasn't just from a need to screw her. It was a far darker need. I clenched my fists. This was the best way. The time would pass.

~ Chapter Twenty-nine ~

Jodie

At the knock on the door, I did a last-minute assessment of my dress. White, slightly lacy, and short. In fact, I'd made very sure it was short with a bodice line that made my breasts stand out. I remembered how much this had turned on Klaus on the night of the party. I was playing with fire doing all this, but too late now.

I closed my eyes a second, then I opened the door.

He took my breath away. Solid man. Blue jeans and a light-brown linen shirt, broad chest, and him. Just him. I think I forgot about needing oxygen for all of five seconds. Unavoidable. Klaus had become my addiction. My nipples tightened, my gut clenched, and I even sighed as I absorbed this wonderful man on my doorstep. This separation he'd devised, it had to go. Had to. I wanted to be his and how could that happen if we were apart?

Then he smiled. "Going to invite me in?"

Uh. "Yes! Come in."

The door clicked shut behind him. Now or never.

I hesitated then took his hand, those thick masculine fingers lying across mine, and without fuss, walked with him down the hallway and then led him into my...our dining room. I looked up at him. The line on his brow deepened as he checked the room, then he centered his gaze on me.

"Where's Adrianna?"

Still holding his hand, I lowered myself to my knees then I bowed my head. "She's not here, Sir. I lied. I lied to get you here."

His sigh was heavy. After his fingers slipped from mine, I felt them bunch in my hair in a familiar stinging grip. My pussy clenched. Whatever it was, habit, an instinctive response, the control spun me into submissiveness. He forced back my head until I looked up into his eyes.

"Why?"

I licked my lips, absorbed in again being under his hand. The room jiggled as he shook my head in emphasis.

"Why, Jodie? Speak."

I shuddered awake. I had to keep above this and be more than a slave if I wanted to sway him.

"Because we're adults, both of us. I know you're afraid you might go too far and hurt me, but that's not going to happen here today, or any day. I agree, we wait for Kat before you let your sadist out. But...I trust you not to."

"You do?" He cocked an eyebrow. "And what if here and now I put you over my knee and spank you for lying? You don't imagine I can hurt you from spanking? I could. Any man is strong enough to."

"But you won't," I whispered.

"What?"

"You won't. You're feeling guilty so you're punishing yourself by keeping away. But it's hurting me to be apart." This time the tears leaked from my eyes. I let them. I let him see.

"Jodie." Again he sighed and his other hand came up and touched the tears. "You look so sad. It's hurting me too. I'm sorry."

I choked for a second, my throat twisting before I could speak. "You already said that, last night. Please? Please? I trust you. I do."

"Too much, perhaps." He let me go, stepped away. "If we're to talk, it'll be outside on your verandah."

My heart leapt. "Okay." Progress. I checked the kettle as we went through the kitchen. The coffee was brewed. "Would you like some?"

"Sure."

So I set out cups and saucers and poured us both a cup. The clink of china, the smell of roasted coffee, and all the little minute details, sent waves of calm filtering through me. And he was here. I could feel his presence in the small kitchen without seeing.

Then he was behind me, his body fitting against the curves of mine as unerringly as the sky fitted against the earth. He kissed the top of my head. My worries drained away and I waited there, absorbing him. Being close again.

"You're beautiful," he murmured, "when you give like this. Just seeing you making coffee for me makes me feel like you need me. Like we suit each other."

I nodded slowly, careful not to bump his mouth, feeling him breathe into my hair. "Me too."

Such a gentle side to his personality, yet it completed him. I loved this part of him too.

"Come." He reached around me and took his own coffee. "Outside."

Smiling, I followed, trying not to let my cup shake on the saucer.

The two-yard-wide verandah out the back of the house ran along outside the kitchen, one story up with stairs, on the left, going down to the back yard. We'd not come out here for the whole month the capture fantasy had run its course. Too public, I guess. The view out across the cliff and the sea was stunning, though. I had a small table and two chairs and we sat opposite each other for a minute or two, sipping coffee and exchanging small talk.

The sea was calm. The cockatoos in the nearby trees were loud. The sky, strangely enough, was blue. Then we fell silent again.

I was nervous but I managed to only play with a strand of my hair, curling it round and round my finger while he observed – sitting like some sort of Buddha made into an accountant with delicious short blond hair.

Waiting…watching. Silent. His eyes had washed to light gray in the sunlight.

"Fuck." I frowned. "Say something."

"No." He leaned in and captured my hair-twirling hand, brought it down to the table and trapped it there under his. "You made this happen. You start, Jodie. You must have thought this through? Explain."

Explain. It had been easy when I was by myself. Take a breath, explain.

"I accept that you're worried you'll hurt me." I nodded a few times. "Moghul told me what happened." I checked his expression but he was merely absorbing my words like a sponge. "But that was in the heat of the moment. I feel like this separation is some weird sort of penance. Punishing us both for one problem is wrong, unnecessary, and...fuck." I bent my head and shoved my hand over my mouth for a second, scowling down at table. "Fuck, this *hurts* us both. Please, please, let us be together."

Unblinking, he stared at me. "Jodie..." He shook his head.

I barreled on, unable to stop my spiel. I had to let this all out or I'd burst. "Okay, so we won't play without Kat for a while. But we can live together. We'll just set boundaries. No S and m activities."

"Maybe you're right. Penance? Maybe I am doing this as penance." He paused a long time as if thinking, then his mouth twisted. "Do you have any idea how tempting it is when I have you naked?"

I smirked. "Perhaps. But after you heard how I'd lied, you didn't spank me, and I'm sure I tempted you."

His eyes fired up. "Yes, you did."

"See."

"But you weren't naked."

"Close. I don't have underwear on." Smiling, I stuck out my tongue tip, touching my upper lip. Then I laughed. "You should see the look on your face."

"That's because the idea of you sitting there without panties has given me an instant hard-on."

"Mmm." My smile widened. "Back on track, though. We can make love without you doing S and m. I know it."

"You do?" He sat back a little. "And you think after all I've done to you that I'll be satisfied with only making love?" His voice trailed off.

"Yes?" I squeaked. Was he saying what I thought he was? That he couldn't do this? Again, tears threatened. I was fragile as butterfly in a hurricane. Another word, the wrong one, and I would cry.

Slowly, he shook his head.

"Oh." I coughed, desperate to hold back those tears. My hand trembled under his.

The coffee cup in front of him was empty. One last gesture. I wanted to do this. To wash it. Then perhaps it would be best if he went. I'd be sad, but I could bear this.

"Let me wash your cup." Washing the dishes for him had become a symbol to me, of submission. I looked at him. "Let me? I need to do this."

His eyes shone. "No."

"Please?" This time tears welled in my eyes. I moved to reach for the cup but he restrained my hand under his.

"Shh. It's going to be okay. No, I won't be satisfied with only making love. Not after having you as my slave. Jodie, you should know how much I liked that – making you my slave. If we were together, I would want that again." His eyes did those small movements as if he were double-checking my expression. His next question ground out harshly. "Would you accept that?"

I couldn't look away. Was this him saying yes? Me, again, at his feet, not having a say in what he did to me? "I would die to have that again. But…" I inhaled. I had to take a stand. "Not always."

"No. Not always. Come here."

He'd changed his mind? Riveted by the possibilities, by the excruciating future that seemed almost *here*, I froze for an instant.

Shaking, I rose and went around the table to stand before him. He smoothed his hands around my back, then down to my thighs and up the sides, slowly raising the dress until he could look beneath at my mons.

"You are indeed naked. Pretty." He cupped my pussy and I gasped at the heat of his palm. "I remember you sitting on Damien at the party. That was so sexy." He paused and studied my face. "The alternative to me hurting you is of course you submitting to me utterly when we're at home and in private. If I want you to lick my shoes or kiss them, or to again sit on the floor at the table while I eat, will you?"

Hell. Why did that arouse me? My clit had instantly perked up. "Yes," I said, hoarsely. "I will. To me, I'm not sure how to explain it, but…" I stared at him pleadingly. "It's my way of loving you."

"I realize that." He sucked in a long shuddering breath, his fingers clamped onto my hip hard, and I heard the sound of his shoe scraping on the timber deck. His eyes were stone.

Whatever he was about to say, must be difficult for him to say. I waited, patient, yet churning up inside with tension.

"I'm not into the word love, Jodie, but you are the only woman for me. Always have been. Always will be. But, I have to ask this. Jodie, you'll trust me?"

"Yes." *God, yes.*

"Okay. I've done my penance. I see your point in that. I want to do small painful things to you that can't escalate into anything dangerous. I am going to trust you to safeword though. Say red if you need to. Okay? But only for pain. No safeword for anything else."

Small and painful. He was back. I didn't bother to ask what he would do. "Red." The word had come out husky and had barely squeezed out my throat. I swallowed. "Yes."

"Good. Excellent. First task." He grinned. "Unzip me and then sit on my cock."

There was nothing before me except his eyes pinning me to the spot and that damn smile. *Fuck. Bastard.*

I didn't want to fail at the first hurdle. I curled my toes, thinking fast. No safeword for this? What about people out here? Someone might see us. My neighbors couldn't, though. Only, perhaps, someone out on a boat. And they'd need a telescope. Unless someone was on the beach below, but even then…

Trust me.

I took a step closer, then I bent over and unbuttoned and slowly unzipped him. I freed his erect cock from his underwear until it stood up where I could see it clearly. The idea of him fucking me outdoors…I was instantly damp. He pushed the table away so there was more space.

"Straddle me. I want to feel your pussy on me. I want to see you, Jodie, in daylight as I penetrate you. Wait, first, wet me with your mouth."

I was already wet enough between my legs, but, he wanted my mouth.

"Yes, Sir." As I lowered myself and knelt, he took my hair, and guided me.

Face turned upward by his hand, I could do nothing as he fingered my lips. "And from now on it's Sir when we are in private."

"Yes, Sir."

Then I let him push my mouth onto his cock. My saliva wet him all along his length and I curled my tongue around him as I went down and came up. I tasted him for the first time in days. The pressure between my legs made me squeeze my thighs together and wriggle my ass. His hand fumbled and slid beneath the bodice of my dress, and over my breast. His finger and thumb clamped onto my nipple. *Uh.* I choked on his cock. The *zing* of the hurt elevated me into another level of excitement. The sadism said *mine* like nothing else.

I'd never worked out why, maybe never would, but I loved that. The multiple tiny pains, his hand in my hair, the sharp ache at my nipple as he tugged and twisted, the dig of his fingers at my hip – all these said I was wanted, taken.

The chair creaked as he shifted and lifted my head away. As my mouth left his erection, a string of saliva wet my chin. I blinked up at him.

"Now sit on me," he growled.

God, yes. I wanted this too. I didn't care who saw. I could *feel* him sliding into me. Mind fogged by desire, I stumbled to my feet, and lifted my dress while he observed my every move.

It was awkward to get my leg on the other side of him but once I had, my legs were far apart and split. My lower lips pulled wide. With his hand at my hip, I directed myself until my entrance poised above, with his tip nudging my center. *Down.* At the exquisite sensation of his cock entering me, I let my head fall forward.

"Go slow," he said, his words husky.

Ah. With my hands braced on his shoulders, I moved down a little, slipping on the wetness from my body. Instinct took me. Without need for thought, my hips rose and fell, sliding me up and down his shaft in tiny distances. I groaned and my breathing hastened.

"More." His hand on my hip clawed into my skin and forced me downward. His cock went farther, farther, until I was seated fully. "Stay still."

"Unh." His pants cloth brushed the back of my thighs. The hard metal zip pressed cold and sharp into my labia. If his balls weren't inside me, they were close. So deep. I fell forward, and nestled my head into the angle of his neck with my hands curled on his chest.

"Good girl," he whispered. "Now, let's discuss business."

"What?" I asked, incredulous, stunned. I could barely put one thought in front of another with him in me.

"Yes, wait. Accommodate me. You'll get used to it." Then he bit and suckled on my neck as if to make it all even more impossible.

But he was right, eventually my thinking processes returned, even if every minute or so I would feel my vagina clamp down on his dick and a shudder possess me.

"Ready to talk?" he asked.

"Mmm. Guess so," I murmured into his skin. I sniffed him and nibbled. His body shook under me as he laughed.

"Good. Now, Jodie. Stop nibbling, by the way." I did. "Say something if you disagree. This is mutual agreement. We are going to live in your house."

I grunted and smelled him some more.

"I will be your Master but no heavy S and m until we sort things out. No impact play at all. No needles, nothing like that. No biting. And that's going to be hard not to do. Your ass…" He groaned and I couldn't help smiling. "Pinching though, nipple clamps, are good. Okay?"

"'Kay." I nodded, my forehead sliding on his muscle. *God.* He felt good inside me.

"You can work locally, I think you said that. Negotiable. Except no tours out of town."

I grunted again. My mind vaguely remembered how I hated tours.

"Documentary shelved. Nothing will go public. We don't need the money."

We? Oh thank God for that. Happy dance. I licked him and tasted just *Him.*

"Fuck, you feel good sweetheart." He thrust up at me, once. "Got all that?"

I wrapped my arms about his shoulders and did my own languid up and down movement, and yes, his cock poked at some wonderful places inside. My eyes rolled back.

"Stop that," he grumbled, and he grabbed my hair with both hands and tilted my head. "Look at me Jodie."

I opened my eyes. Inches away, his stared into mine.

"Tell me, Jodie. Who owns you? Are you mine? Because I think you are. I think you're fucking mine."

I swam inside the world of his eyes. "Yes," I croaked. "I am yours, Sir."

"Of course you are." He shook my head a little and lowered his voice to the level of a wolf prowling in the darkness. "Now, kiss me, then you can go do my dishes. And when you have done that, return and we will finish this."

That small statement thrummed into me. "Thank you, Sir." I met his lips with mine, and we softly kissed. The possession – his hands in my hair, his cock inside me, and his mouth on me – this unraveled my universe and bound me irrevocably to him.

And I...I was precisely where I belonged.

The End

Other Books by Cari Silverwood

The Badass Brats Series

The Dom with a Safeword

The Dom on the Naughty List

The Dom with the Perfect Brats

The Steamworks Chronicles Series

Iron Dominance

Lust Plague

Steel Dominance

The Rough Surrender Series

Rough Surrender

Cataclysm Blues Series

Cataclysm Blues

Others

31 Flavors of Kink

Three Days of Dominance

www.CariSilverwood.net

www.facebook.com/cari.silverwood

The Dom with the Perfect Brats

Book 3 in the Badass Brats series

Godfrey Cross is a big, tattooed Dom with no tolerance for brats. But when he meets Gemma and Izzy, two mouthy vanilla girls, he begins to see their charm.

These bratty girls seem more into each other than into him and he wonders if he's wasting his time. Yet despite the clash between his strict version of BDSM and their rebellious natures, he finds himself growing to love them.

When his need for control tears their relationship apart, they must learn to compromise or they will lose each other. People might not be perfect, but could these two be perfect for him?

* * *

When Gemma and Izzy express interest in his upcoming sale, Godfrey Cross invites them to his Goth clothes store after hours. The girls have been teasing him and only have a vague idea as to how far Cross will go…

Excerpt

The next time they came out, giggling and flushed, they wore matching black PVC dresses with black studded leather collars. Gemma's expression was downright naughty, and Izzy looked smug. Cross immediately imagined bringing them into the club like that, on a tandem leash, but freshly spanked and biddable. He stifled a hiss as his arousal evaded his control.

"So are you two a matched set now?" He arched a brow.

Gemma bit her lip then prowled over to him, dragging Izzy in her wake. "I think he likes these, Izzy. What is it, knuckle-dragger? The twin thing? The collar thing? Are we making you think bad thoughts?"

"I warned you I'm no gentleman." Cross adjusted himself through his jeans without any attempt at being subtle.

They both looked amused. Not easily shocked, for vanilla girls.

"So if we touched you, would you fall at our feet and worship us?" Gemma looked at Cross speculatively.

"Maybe I should tie your hands together to avoid that?" he growled. Girls didn't talk to him like this. They ducked their heads and did what they were told. He had to fight down mild annoyance. This girl wasn't his... yet. If she was, she'd be clutching her sore ass by now, with fat tears rolling down her cheeks. His heart beat faster. This time he didn't hesitate to get into her personal space as he loomed over her. Izzy, who she still clutched, got the same view. Now both of them looked up at him with wide eyes. Even vanilla girls understood this body language. Godfrey Cross was not a man to fuck with.

After a short silence, Izzy lifted her hands, giving him a sassy grin that paled compared to Gemma's prior challenge. "I double-dare you."

He looked down. Offering her wrists. Brat. Gemma snickered, obviously thinking she was safe.

Without pause, he pulled Gemma's arms behind Izzy's back. "Stay." He grabbed Izzy's wrists and put them behind her too, then zip-tied their same wrists together. They'd actually cooperated. He stepped back and admired his work. They were stuck with Gemma hugging Izzy, and Izzy unable to get away. Nice. He generally preferred leather cuffs or rope for real bondage, but the zip ties would do.

"Hey!" Both girls protested briefly, testing their bonds. The sound of PVC sliding along PVC was sexy. And the collars. Nothing was hotter than a woman wearing a collar – except maybe for a woman wearing *his* collar.

"Oh no! What's to become of us, dear Izzy? Now we're totally at his mercy." So much sarcasm in such a little girl. They looked at him expectantly. Despite the brave words, Gemma seemed unsettled. "I bet he's like every other straight guy I know and he's hoping we'll kiss."

Izzy laughed breathlessly. Though Gemma watched him, she was staring in fascination at Gemma's mouth.

"A couple of straight, good girls like you? I wouldn't put money on it," he mocked.

Gemma's brows shot up. "Good girl? You wish." Her face swung to Izzy, who looked at her with trepidation and even flinched the tiniest amount.

As Gemma leaned toward her, pulling her closer, Izzy tried to squirm away. "Don't," she squeaked. Gemma ignored her and pressed her lips to the girl's in a chaste way, then withdrew.

Cross laughed. "You're a virgin, Gemma? That's all that kiss said to me."

She glared at him, not noticing the way Izzy's tits heaved or her helpless look of arousal.

Gemma snorted and turned back to her new friend. Challenge accepted. She pulled Izzy closer, with the girl whimpering but not trying hard to stop her. Slowly Gemma leaned in until their lips almost touched. Her tongue tip traced the seam of Izzy's lips, teasing, testing, like she wanted to see what Izzy would do.

Fucking hot. He resisted grabbing her hair and instructing. If the building had fallen down, he might not have noticed. *This* was better than his daydreams.

Gemma bit the girl's bottom lip – he could see the tug of skin as she pulled. When Izzy gasped she slipped her tongue into her mouth and started to kiss her in earnest. Izzy submitted, relaxing into her arms then kissing her back. When, at last, Gemma pulled away, Izzy mewled, trying to follow her and not let it end.

Now that, *that*, was fucking hot.

They were both pink and blotchy, breathing hard, looking at him. Gemma exhaled shakily. "Happy now?"

He couldn't stay out of this anymore – all of his Dom instincts were pacing the cage, trying to escape. Vanilla or not? Time to find out.

Drawing himself up, he towered over them and growled. "Again."

"What?" Gemma whispered, brow furrowed.

He glowered down at her, almost touching them he was standing so close. He ran a finger under the collar she'd put on as a joke, slowly, letting her feel the pressure. "I didn't tell you to stop, girl. Do it again."

Izzy backpedaled, almost pulling Gemma off her feet. He stopped Izzy with a hand on the nape of her neck, and steadied Gemma with a hand under her elbow.

"Stop trying to get away, Izzy. I know you like this." He waited a second to let the idea sink in. "Just let it happen. You can blame me later, if you need to." He held her with thumb and forefinger wrapped around her neck, over the collar. He stroked gently with his thumb. Though trembling, she didn't argue.

When he looked back to Gemma, she stared him in the eye. She didn't want to like this, but somewhere in there, deep down, she did.

"Do it. Now."

He could feel the heat coming off of her. She liked this, even if she wouldn't say so. And neither of them had told him to fuck off or untie them.

After one, long, exasperated sigh, Gemma took up the kiss where she'd left off.

He placed a gentle hand on the back of her neck too. She tried to jerk away but groaned into Izzy's mouth. Small noises of pleasure gave way to frustrated moans from Izzy. Somehow his hands had entangled in their hair, and soon he couldn't help himself and started controlling their movements. The writhing of their bodies, their sounds and the way they'd wrapped themselves around each other –

fuck. His cock pressed hard against his jeans, not used to being denied for so long. He was surprised his dick hadn't detached and gone stomping through the store like Godzilla through Tokyo.

www.CariSilverwood.net

www.facebook.com/cari.silverwood

Made in the USA
Las Vegas, NV
31 January 2022

42690595R10115